Every Girl Needs ...
By: Amber Shanel

Dedication

This one is dedicated to all of those who believed in me and also those who support me, I love you all! I hope you enjoy!

Acknowledgments

First off I want to thank God for blessing me with such an art as this. I truly am grateful for it. At times I feel as if I'm not a good writer but I look to all my supporters and they give me the strength I need. To Talehia for giving a youngin' a chance. When I first got into this game my sister, "Boss Lady" helped me with a lot. We stayed up numerous of nights talking and I just want to thank her for her time. The one and only Talehia Mccants. My little sister who I hit up at any time of the day (literally) so I can complain to her lol Joya, love you boo!

With my long absence from the book game, I want to thank all the readers for giving me another chance to showcase my talents it truly means a lot.

My mother for asking me what book am I putting out, she stays on me as much as anyone else does and I thank her for that.

Every member of my 'Book Palace' everyone is so active and I love them all dearly. If I needed a test reader they never mind!

All the inboxes, wall post, even the text etc they do not go unnoticed at all!

To le squad Talehia Presents Publication; continue grinding love you all too!

If I missed anyone PLEASE blame it on my mind and not my heart

#RIPGranddaddy

Follow my Instagram: @ohshesamber

Follow my twitter: @ambershanelx

My Facebook: Amber Shanel

'Like' My Author Page: Author Amber Shanel

Join My Reader's Group on Facebook: Amber Shanel's Book Palace

- Amber Shanel

Chapter One

KNOCK! KNOCK!

Little did Moisha know, her best friend was banging as if she was the police at her door. Moisha was knocked out and planned on getting about a three hour nap. She had just graduated from college with an English degree, so she felt as if she deserved every bit of sleep she could get.

Zara continued to bang and soon, Moisha was up and mad. Her feet touched the floor, and she grabbed her house coat off the end of her bed and fumed out her room down the hall to the door.

"What bitch?!" she said, as she opened the door. Zara laughed and invited herself in. "No… really, what do you want?" Moisha asked and then crossed her arms over one another, waiting to see what Zara had to say for herself.

"Bitch," Zara started, "you just graduated from college with a damn 4.2 GPA and you in here sleep. What type of shit?" Zara asked and Moisha shrugged.

"What you expect me to do? Go out tonight or something? Get drunk? Get high? Do all the shit I didn't do in college?" Moisha challenged her. "I'll just wait until my birthday when I turn twenty-four," she added in, with an eye roll.

Zara laughed a little. "Your birthday is like in two months; that's too far and I mean I think it would be nice if you would go out and celebrate your accomplishment." Zara cheesed.

"Z, I am not going any fucking where. Now, get the fuck up out of my house," Moisha said. She then went into the kitchen to get something to drink. Zara just rolled her eyes and did as she was told; in the process, she slammed the door. Moisha smirked to herself and went back into her room.

Her family wanted to take her out to eat so that was basically all she was going to do. Moisha came from a middle class family. They Jones' weren't wealthy at all but all five of them had what they needed. Moisha knew that her parents didn't have the money to put her through college, so luckily, she was about to get a four year scholarship that she didn't take for granted at all. So, throughout college, Moisha was about her shit, molding her into the person she is today.

Moisha graduated yesterday and today was Friday. It was going on five o'clock and Moisha's parents and other family members wanted to meet at Maggiano's at seven for dinner. She figured she might as well start to get ready because her mother was a stickler for being on time and Moisha knows that she takes a long time to get ready. She placed her drink down on her nightstand then went into her walk-in closet. Going through rack after rack, trying to figure out what to wear, was pure hell. Moisha had so many damn clothes and on top of that, she didn't have no idea of what to wear. She ran her hands through her freshly permed hair and sighed dramatically.

"Think. Momo, think," Moisha coached herself.

Soon, Moisha laid out three outfits: a black jumpsuit with a deep v-cut, a jean pencil skirt with a coral buttoned up shit that you are able to tie in the front at the end, and lastly, a red Bodycon dress. Moisha then hoped into the shower.

As she showered, she thought about all the longs nights of studying and to say that they finally paid off is an understatement. She finally accomplished a goal in her life. Getting her degree, she wanted to teach high school English but she wanted to be an editor for this fashion magazine first. Moisha honestly had so many things she wanted to do, but she knew she had to take it day by day.

Moisha was now out the shower and dry. She lotioned her body and then sprayed it with body mist. After putting on her undergarments, she went to her bed. Looking at the three outfits, she quickly put on the jean pencil skirt and coral shirt. Moisha didn't quite button the shirt up all the way, she did it right before you could see her cleavage. Walking back into her room, she picked up the hot flat iron and began to straighten her hair so it could be fresh. Moisha flipped her hair when she was done, obviously feeling herself. Turning around, Moisha had to see how the back looked. She wasn't the smallest girl, but Moisha definitely was blessed in all the right places.

After putting on gold jewelry, she walked into her closet to get her shoes, which were Gold caged heels that went up a little bit before ankle. Once she got her purse and phone, she looked at the time. She had about twenty minutes to get there.

***

"MY BABY!" Faith, Moisha's mother, said as she saw Moisha walked in their direction.

"Hey mommy." Moisha smiled.

"Hello baby, congratulations once again," Marc, her father, said.

Moisha look at the table and saw her little sister. "Myaaaaa," Moisha said and kissed her, as she sat beside her.

"Hey Momo." Mya smiled. Mya was a junior in high school and favored Moisha so much, it was crazy.

"Where is Mat?" Moisha asked as she looked around for her brother.

"He said he'll be here," Faith replied.

Mathew was married with two kids, so they figured that was the hold up. He didn't often participate in family events but this one was very important.

"So, have you found a job?" Marc asked.

To be quite honest, Moisha had a job but she didn't want to work at the moment. She just wanted to chill out but she knew her parents weren't going to have that at all.

"Yeah…" Moisha replied with a smile

"When do you start?" Her dad asked again. Moisha hated to lie to her dad but sometimes, you have to do what you have to do.

"Um, I'm not even sure yet. I have to see," She said and she was saved by the waitress asking for their drink orders. In the mist of the waitress, Marc, his wife, and two kids showed up.

After everyone got acquainted, Marc spoke up. "Congratulations again Momo. Now, you do not have an excuse to babysit Ayanna and Tianna," he said, referring to his twin daughters that were six years old and everyone laughed.

"Do you plan on staying in Memphis?" he asked once again.

"For the most part… yeah," Moisha replied. She has been here all her life and didn't really plan on relocating. Growing up in a very close knit family, Moisha always wanted to live her life the same. She wanted to go to school, getting the necessary credentials to do what she love and making good money in the process, and then find the man of her dreams, falling in love and living happily ever after. It could all be so simple but for Moisha, it wasn't.

As everyone at the table was talking, her phone slightly vibratd, indicating she had received a test message. She then grabbed her phone, looking to see it was from Zara.

Bitch. I have moves, please get out of the bed and come out tonight.

Unknowingly, Moisha smacked her teeth out loud. "Excuse me?" her mother asked.

"Sorry... everyone," Moisha apologized. She definitely didn't mean to do that out loud like that. They all continued eating, talking amongst each other. As for Moisha, of course, she was eating but she was thinking about going out. She couldn't even remember when the last time she went out.

"Mya, what I tell you about elbows on the table?" Faith streaked. Mya rolled her eyes slightly and huffed as she readjusted herself.

"What was that?" Faith asked.

Mya shook her head. "Nothing" Mya was always the problem child. She had her own way of doing things, and Moisha couldn't lie and say that she wasn't like that when she was Mya's age. Mya and Moisha were so much alike; it was ridiculous.

Dinner was finally over and Moisha was on her way back home. Moisha grabbed her phone and dialed Zara's number as she kept her focus on the road.

"Hello...bitch," Zara said into the phone.

"What's up? I decided that I'll go out tonight," Moisha replied, siding with Zara. Little did she know, Zara was cheesing on the other end of the phone.

"So, what's the move?" Moisha asked.

"EJ house," Zara said. "Meet me there in like ten minutes."

EJ was Zara's boo thing but they weren't exactly together. They been off and on for about two years. Moisha has been over there plenty of times and looked to EJ as a brother.

"Bitch, I need to change my clothes!" Moisha said.

"Noooo, you probably look good, so just come on. It's just EJ and his boys. No one to look all cute for," Zara said and Moisha exhaled, going into the direction of EJ's place. He lived on the other side of Memphis, close to the hood.

"But you probably look cute," Moisha whined.

"No, I really do not. See you there, boo," Zara said then ended the call. She then tossed her phone in the cup holder and continued focusing on the road to EJ's.

She finally made it and decided to park on the curb, in front of the mailbox. Just as she was checking to see how she was looking in the mirror, Zara was pulling into the driveway, blasting music how she usually does. Moisha hopped out of her 2013 Jeep and proceeded to the front door.

"You do look cute," Zara said, matter-of-factly.

"I guess," Moisha replied.

Zara took out her key to EJ's door and went ahead and opened the door for her and Moisha.

"We here!" Zara's loud ass yelled.

"Z," Moisha snapped, after she was done yelling.

The house smelled like pure marijuana but the two of them knew that was nothing new. All EJ did was smoke weed; he really didn't have a life but Zara saw the better in him.

"Momoooo." He smiled, coming to hug them.

EJ was tall, about 6'2, caramel with shoulder length dreads. He wasn't bad looking at all, he was just child minded, which Zara didn't like at all. "Move," Zara said and walked straight to the living room.

"What I do?" he asked Moisha. She shrugged and followed her best friend. There were bottles of Grey Goose, Amsterdam, and Hennessy on the table. Zara was a Henny fanatic, so she opened the bottle and took a cup from the stack getting some. Two other men came into the room that were not EJ and Moisha quickly observed them.

She began feeling something won't right. She looked over at Zara. "Babe, I'm going to go-"

"No, do not leave me," Zara stressed, as she filled up another cup.

"Slow down on the drinks Z-"

Just as the last syllable came out of Moisha's mouth, a shot came through the window, resulting in all the glass shattering.

"Get down!!!" one of the random two men yelled.

"What the fuck!" Moisha screamed out in anger. The time she decides to go out and do something, some shit pops off.

The shots came and Moisha felt as if she was in World War II. Luckily, she wasn't that big and was able to fit under the coffee table. Moisha was scared but pissed more than anything. She heard something fall down and then everything went quiet. Her breathing calmed down back to normal and she figured she should give it another minute or so before looking.

"Look around the house, I do not think anyone is here," a smooth, husky voice said. Moisha plans to get up from the table was changed; she was going to stay her ass down there.

"Nigga, I think the cops coming," another voice spoke.

"Yeah, yeah, keep watch out. I'll look my damn self," the voice replied. Moisha could hear his steps wandering over to where she was. She tensed up then paused her breathing, so he wouldn't hear. Moisha slightly turned to the left and could see the black Gucci Loafers.

"Whoever this is…he got money," Moisha said in her head, she dare not say it out loud though.

"Really," he said and squatted down to Moisha's level.

"Damn," she cursed under her breath.

"Get up," he said and she did as told, shaking the entire time.

Prince looked at Moisha as she did so. He couldn't lie, she had a fat ass, but there was business to handle. He wouldn't dare hurt her, but he could use her. His mind focused back on Moisha; she dusted her clothes off and Prince stared in the process. She was beyond beautiful.

"Business…Prince. Business," he coached himself in his head.

"Come with me," he spoke and turned around, hoping she was going to follow. Moisha stood back and took a look at the house; whoever came in tore it up to pieces. EJ or Zara was nowhere to be found. She checked her phone and no notifications, which was weird.

"It was more of a demand. You do not have a choice," Prince mentioned over his shoulder, once he saw that Moisha wasn't following him. Moisha quickly left, once she heard the sirens. She didn't have time for answering questions about shit she ain't know about.

"The police are coming, so you and I have to go," he said.

"There's my car, so I'll go," Moisha pointed and said.

Prince chuckled. "See. I'm trying to be nice. Get in this damn car, so we can go. You have to come with me. Are we clear?" Prince asked, not really caring about her response.

Moisha was shaken up. The fact that this random ass man that she didn't know just told her what to do and was able to shut her up, surprised her a little bit. They both got into the car and Prince sped off. He knew that when the police came, she was going to look suspicious from the jump. Yeah. Moisha left her car but that could always be replaced or Prince could get it towed to wherever she needed it to be at.

"So, who are you?" Moisha asked after texting Zara for the hundredth time.

"Prince," was all he said because that was all she needed to know. "And you are?" he asked in return.

"Moisha... so what happened back there and where is my friend?"

Prince was too busy trying to focus on getting to his apartment and find shit out. A lot of his guys took care of the people that were in the house and to be honest, he didn't really know there was anyone else in the house other than EJ and his two niggas.

"Your friend... who?" Prince replied.

"Zara... about 5'7" or 5'6", light skin," she said and Prince looked as if he didn't know in hell what she was talking about.

"I'mma be honest with you, ma. I didn't see no other female in there with you but here's what I'll do. I'll hit up my niggas and ask... okay?" he said sincerely.

"What the fuck." Moisha huffed, she began to feel like a bad friend.

Before Moisha knew it, they pulled up into a gated apartment community. She knew of this place but never came because this was on another side of Memphis.

Prince inputted a code and the gate opened. The apartments were beyond luxurious, so Moisha was liking what she was seeing.

"So, how long do I have to stay with you?" Moisha asked out of curiosity. "Why can't I just go home?" she asked in a 'duh' tone.

"Because, I do not trust you," Prince replied simply. "I do not know you or nothing. Just chill out ma. I promise I won't hurt you, tryna' just clear some shit out. Now, just make yourself comfortable. Do you want anything, water, juice?" he asked, showing his southern hospitality.

"No. No thank you," Moisha said and sat down on the couch. Prince directed her how to work the TV and soon, she had on re-runs of Bad Girls Club. She was in her own zone.

Prince was on the phone and from time to time, he would look over at Moisha. She was completely knocked out but just to be on the safe side, he took his conversation into one of the two bedrooms.

***

"Tone. You killed her! What the fuck man? This like the hundredth time you did this bullshit" Lonzo said, referring to Zara. Little did she know, she was in the basement of a trap house, tied up like a prisoner.

"No nigga. Her pulse is still… ya' know. Pulsing!" Tone exaggerated.

Lonzo took a look and nodded in satisfaction. Prince was over the whole operation of raiding EJ's crib and he didn't want any witnesses, so little miss light skin right here had to die. Just as Tone was adjusting the ropes, in came Prince.

"What's good boss?" Lonzo asked.

Prince looked at an unconscious Zara and all he had to say was, "Untie her."

"Wh-" Just as Tone was about to ask why, Prince shut him down real quick with a simple hand motion. Lonzo and Tone began to untie Zara and she was completely knocked out. Her body was limp. They took her body up to the living room and laid her down on the couch.

Tone went about his business but since Lonzo was closer to Prince, he decided to stay and see what's up.

"Was there anyone else in the house?" Lonzo asked him.

Prince lit the freshly rolled blunt. "Yeah."

"Well, where are they?"

"My house. I'll explain later," he replied.

Chapter Two

A quiet yawn slipped from Moisha's mouth as she sat up in the couch. She looked over to her left and saw Zara laid out on the couch.

"Bitch!!!!" Moisha smiled. She began shaking Zara and slowly but surely, Zara woke up wondering where the hell she was at.

"Mo… where are we?" she asked, then coughed.

"Some nigga named Prince's house; are you okay?" Moisha asked Zara. She was just happy her best friend was okay, well at least she looked okay.

Zara and Moisha were both on the couch in Prince's living room. Moisha picked up her phone thinking it was on but it was dead. "Shit," she huffed.

"Let me go see where this nigga is because I'm hungry and I need to charge my damn phone," Moisha spat, then got up from the couch.

She began to yell Prince's name as she walked throughout the house. As she walked down the hallway, she heard movement coming from the room at the end, so she began to go to that room. Since the door was slightly cracked opened, Moisha took it upon herself to go inside the room.

"Prince? Oh shit, I'm so sorry," Moisha said, once she realized that Prince only had a towel wrapped around the lower part of his body. Moisha couldn't help but to stare at his built frame. The water droplets intensified his smooth chocolate skin.

"It's alright," he replied with a chuckled because he knew for a fact, Moisha was looking at him.

"I'll be in the living room," Moisha said with her head down. As she was walking back to the living room, she had to fan herself. She was getting hot. Once Moisha was back in the living room, she gave Zara the 411 and Zara then asked when they would be able to go home. Moisha had no clue and that is exactly what she told Zara.

"I've been calling EJ nonstop and he is not even answering. He left you and I in the middle of some drug shit, like what the fuck!" Zara screamed out in tears.

EJ obviously just showed how much he loved Zara yesterday. She knew that she needed to leave his no good ass alone but the heart tends to want what it cannot handle.

Prince made his way up to the living room, so he could give Moisha and Zara both a run down about how he was going to spare their lives.

"He fine as hell," Zara tried to whisper but Prince heard her. Moisha nudged her.

"Anyways," Prince chuckled. "I wanted to let the both of you know that I am sparing your lives and that you can go home. Under one condition. I will have two of my men watching and following you two for the next sixty days. You know, just to see if you dumb enough to tell any information," Prince explained.

"As long as whoever is watching me stays out of my damn house and personal space. We got a deal," Zara said.

"Um. This wasn't a proposal," Prince said and Zara got quiet. Moisha, on the other hand, was just happy to go home.

"What about our cars Prince?" Moisha asked.

"They're actually outside and your belongings are in them. Just remember what I said about not saying shit and you two are good to go," Prince said.

***

Moisha was finally home, trying to decide what to do with her life. The magazine she had an internship with for the last two years offered her a full time job starting in July, which was in two months. Basically, Moisha had two months to do whatever the hell she wanted to do, then get to business in July.

Once she was settled in, able to charge her phone, and just rejuvenate herself, she hopped in the shower. After she took a well needed shower, she began taking care of some more hygiene and then put her hair up in a bun. Moisha was about to spend the day with her younger sister, Mya. It was well needed; she always wanted to maintain a good relationship with her siblings.

Moisha dressed in a tight, above the knee, grey dress. It was a very fitted and expressed her shape. She decided on wearing her black, high top Converse and carried along a Levi jean jacket, just in case it got cold. The moment she got done getting all together, she was out.

The whole way to her parents' house, she was blasting Tink, thinking about how fast these two months are about to go. She was going to be working and she knew it, so she wanted to make the best out of these two months and just have fun spending time with her friends and family.

She then pulled into her parents' driveway, cutting out her car, then using her key to go inside.

"Mo is here!" Moisha shouted, then went over to the table by the door to see if any mail was for her. It wasn't, so she went ahead and went upstairs to Mya's room.

"I'm coming in," Moisha said, then barged right on in.

"Mo… when you get here?" Mya asked, cutting off her loud music.

Moisha looked around the teenager's room, which reminded her of how her room was when she was sixteen. "Like now. What's up?" Moisha asked, sitting down on Mya's bed. Mya was on twitter, like always, tweeting about nothing. Moisha left Mya's room, then went to her parents' room to see that no one was there. She then came to the conclusion that no one was in the house but Mya.

"Where's mom and dad?" Moisha asked.

"Uhhhh, dad had to go in the office and mom is doing her Saturday morning errands. You know. Ain't nothing change," Mya said, as she got up from her bed and put on black leggings with a grey Nike shirt, along with her cool grey 9's.

"What we doing today? You know we have to hang out." Mya laughed, as she was flat ironing her hair.

"Well, I need a fill-in, so we can go to the nail salon and I guess whatever you want to do next," Moisha replied.

"Yassss, mani pedi's!" Mya rejoiced, then got her purse and left her room. Mya followed in suit.

"So, you have a boyfriend yet?" Mya asked her big sister.

"No Mya. Why?" Moisha asked back, wondering why the hell was her younger sister worried about whether she had a boyfriend or not.

"Just wondering. You need a man though." Mya laughed, exciting the house. They both got into Moisha's car, making their way to the nail salon.

Mya's question did linger in Moisha's mind for a bit though. Moisha had one boyfriend. Well, she didn't even want to count that nigga as her boyfriend because after he took her virginity, he just disappeared. She remembers everything vividly; it was spring semester of her freshmen year of college and a junior had been wanting to talk to her for the longest. Moisha was always on her shit and wanted it to remain that way, so she didn't really pay it any mind. Until he, James, asked her out on a date. After a few dates, Moisha found herself liking him. She liked him so much; she was willing to give him her most prized possession.

She hasn't spoken to him since and she beat herself up about it because you always wanted to give your virginity to a guy well worth it and James wasn't.

Soon as Moisha knew it, she was pulling into a parking spot in front of the nail salon. It was a nice sunny day, so Moisha put her jacket in the backseat, then got out the car, locking it. Mya opened the door for her and Moisha to go in. The nail salon wasn't as packed as she thought it was, so that was a plus.

"Hello. How may help you?" a Chinese women asked in her thick Chinese accent.

"A fill-in, pedicure…" Moisha then looked at Mya, as to what she was getting.

"Manicure and pedicure." Mya smiled.

Two hours later, the girls had their nails done and were ready to go get something to eat. As Mya dried her feet a little more, Moisha went up to the desk to pay for her nails.

"Um ma'am, already been paid for," the lady said.

Moisha scrunched up her eyebrows and asked, "Who?" By now, Mya was standing next to her being nosey.

The lady pointed to a man who was standing outside the nail salon on the phone. "Have a nice day," Moisha said, then exited the salon.

The Chinese woman smiled and Mya smirked. "Girl, we just got a free trip to the nail salon," she said while laughing.

"Just because it's free doesn't mean it's actually free though. Come on," Moisha said, then motioned towards the door to talk to the man. He was on the phone and she didn't really want to seem rude but she couldn't help it.

"Excuse me." He turned around slightly. "Hold on, I'm going to call you back," he said, then ended the call.

Moisha thought her eyes were fucking with her. She didn't usually do light skin males, but the one currently standing in her face was a goddess in an Armani suit. He had to be about 6'2", slim and perfect white teeth. His hair was a low top fade, not to mention the diamond earring that shined from his left ear.

"I just wanted to say thank you for paying for my sister and I's nails," Moisha said nervously. She couldn't help but to be nervous in his presence. He demanded submission.

"It's no problem at all sweetheart. I was watching you as you got out the car that is because you caught my eye. I just wanted to let you know how beautiful you are," he spoke with smoothness dripping from his voice.

"Awh, well I'm Moisha." She smiled. Mya snatched her keys, then got in the car. She didn't feel like waiting and watching her flirt.

"And I'm Wesley; it is such a pleasure to meet you. Can I please have your number?" he asked Moisha, giving her his million dollar smile. Moisha would have been a fool to say no. So, there she was outside of a nail salon, giving the man that paid for she and her sister's nails her number.

"I'll be contacting you very soon," he said, then they said their goodbyes and departed.

Moisha got into the car, looking at Mya. "See, I told you just because it's free doesn't mean it's really free!" Moisha spoke, referring to her number she had to give up just because he paid for their nails.

"Except for them samples at Sam's on Saturday mornings," Mya joked, making her and Moisha laugh. "But Mo, he was fine as helllllllllllllllllllllll," Mya exaggerated.

"Oh. I know, which is why slid him my number," Moisha said, smirking.

"Okay 'free'." Mya laughed and so did Moisha.

***

Prince walked into one of his many trap houses; he wanted to check in with the men that had been watching Zara and Moisha, just to see if anything fishy has happened. He wanted to always keep tabs on them. Shit happened too fast out here and he wanted to be prepared for anything that life threw at him.

He went into the living room and called the two of them in. In total, there were four men being a watchful eye; two for Zara and two for Moisha; one in the day and one in the night.

"What's up boss?" JJ spoke while sitting down. He had just got done with his watchful eye shift with Moisha.

"So, anything strange been happening with Moisha?" Prince asked, getting straight to the point. There was no need to beat around the bush. Prince was a pretty straight forward person.

"No sir. To be quite honest, she does not do shit," he expressed.

Prince stroked his goatee. "So, she seems like a good girl huh?" Prince asked him for his person records. He wanted to know the type of woman Moisha was.

JJ nodded real fast. "Hell yeah. The strangest thing I could say she did today was give some nigga her number and that's literally it," JJ replied.

"Her number huh?" Prince asked for clarification. Prince did, in fact, have his eye on Moisha but with a woman like her, you had to take your time with your move. Sometimes, you just had to chill, see what type of woman she is, then go for the goal and that was what Prince was exactly doing.

Prince was twenty-seven and hoes were played out to him. He knew, sooner or later, it was going to be time for him settle down and shit. He wasn't getting any younger, so he knew he needed to find someone true, loyal, freaky, and wife material. After getting the 411 on Zara, Prince left the house, going to his soul food carryout place downtown. Prince didn't really do much cooking. He could cook though but tonight, he didn't really feel like it. He got on the highway, turning up the radio. Young Thug's *Best friend* blasted throughout his car. Prince was in the zone. He got off at his desired exit going towards the soul food place. Once the dirty money came in quicker than he could count, it this was his first investment. A soul food restaurant in memory of his mother. Business was too good; it was a very popular place, no matter the race, and Prince loved that. He even named it after his mother, *Heaven's Kitchen.*

Prince parked then got out looking at the place, nodding his head in satisfaction. The moment he stepped inside, he went straight to the back, of course, hearing the workers greet him on his way there.

As Prince was in the back, in came Moisha and her sister Mya. "I already know what I'm getting," Mya trailed off with a smirk.

"Which is?" Moisha asked.

"Rice and cabbage. So, I can get an ass so fat, he wanna grab it," Mya said and Moisha instantly laughed.

"Well, you came to the right place," Moisha replied, as they both sat at the bar so they could look at a menu. *Heaven's Kitchen* was the name of the place and Moisha loved it. The food was divine and for a good price, it was pretty popular in town.

"How y'all doing? You dining in or taking out?" a server came up to the bar and asked them.

"We're going to take out," Moisha replied.

"Alright, just let me know when you two are ready." The lady walked away with a smile and Moisha turned slightly to her left to see a person she thought she wasn't going to even see again. Like their first acquaintance, Moisha was mesmerized by him. The way he carried himself, how he demanded respect in any room he walked in, no, it definitely had to be how he said her name. It was Prince and she was definitely surprised to see him here.

"How are you?" Prince asked, snapping Moisha out of her thoughts.

"Surprised you even remember my name," she said smiling but was serious as hell

"How can I not forget," he said with a chuckle. He wouldn't dare forget the name of someone so beautiful.

"My name is Mya," Mya spoke with a smile, interjecting.

"Yeah, that's my little sister," Moisha said, then kicked her for being rude. In return, Mya bucked at her.

"You must have looked like that when you were younger," Prince said.

"She wish," Mya taunted. Moisha gave her a look. "Okay, I'll hush now." She giggled.

Prince motioned her to sit down at a booth across the bar. Moisha, of course, accepted. They both sat on opposite sides. "So, how have you been?"

"Good. Just being watched and followed," she said, referring to the man that Prince had watching her. He chuckled but that didn't mean he was going to tell his men to stop.

"Sounds good to me, did you pay yet?" he asked and Moisha shook her head.

Prince nodded his head. "Well, it's on me. I'll tell my girl I got y'all food"

"Your girl? Girlfriend?" Moisha asked, surprised. She honestly hoped he didn't have a girlfriend.

"No... this is my place," he said, matter-of-factly.

"You. Own. Heaven's?" Moisha asked with wide eyes.

He nodded. "Yeah. Heaven is my mother that passed about five years ago. She loved cooking, so I got her old recipes and in memory of her, this was the outcome." He smiled, proud of himself. He knew his mother would be proud of him also.

"Sorry to hear that but that is so awesome, wow Prince." Moisha smiled, still hyped. She wanted people in her life that was doing good shit for themselves. To be quite honest, she wanted a man that had shit going for himself. Success was very attractive to both Prince and Moisha.

"So, what's your occupation?" Prince asked. He sat his things down because he felt as if they both were about to be here for a little while.

"Well, I just graduated from college with a degree in English. I'm not employed now but in two months, I'll be an Editor for this Urban Magazine."

"Out of Memphis?"

"Yes sir." Moisha smiled.

"Wow, look at you," he said with a smile, "So, who's the lucky man? I know there has to be one," he said.

"You cannot be serious," Moisha suggested. Moisha had absolute no type of man in any way, shape, form, or fashion.

"But I am," Prince replied with a very serious look.

Moisha sighed, thinking about how she doesn't have a 'boo' in her life. "There is no man in my life but my father and my brother," Moisha replied honestly.

Moisha and Prince conversed for a while and Prince learned quite a bit about Moisha. The same with Prince. Moisha learned that Prince really didn't have anyone, well he had his mother but she died five years ago. She was really the only thing he cared about in this world, so once he left, he was really on his 'fuck the world' shit. He knew sooner or later, he was going to have to settle down and rest that mentality because it wasn't really a good look.

At this point in his life, he was just focused on his money. Yeah, he wanted to settle down soon but he couldn't just do that with anyone. To Prince, most of the females he encountered wanted to trap him and take his money, but he could see that Moisha was different. Moisha was independent.

"It was good talking with you, Prince," Moisha said after Prince told her he had to go, unfortunately.

"The pleasure was all mines," Prince said with a smile. Moisha smiled and then he turn around to leave. It concerned Moisha that he didn't ask for her number. She pushed the thought to the back of her head and went over to the bar where her sister was eating the food that came.

"Well, damn Mya," Moisha said with a laugh. She grabbed the bag with her to go tray in it.

"What? You was talking to that man and the food came, so I took it upon myself to get busy" She smiled, then asked one of the servers to dispose of her tray. Mya hopped down the bar stool, following Moisha to the car.

"I see you, sis." Mya smirked. "Getting all the juice!"

Chapter Three

A Couple Days Later…

Moisha realized that she hadn't spoken to Zara in about three days. Usually, she would pop up or at least text. Not communicating was definitely unlike Zara. Moisha reached over, snatching her phone off the charger and quickly going to Zara's contact. She waited for Zara to answer, it was taking forever. Just as Moisha was about to hang up, Zara answered.

"Yeah?"

Moisha was taken back by her answer. "Yea?! Girl, I haven't spoken to you in like three days. What's up with that?" Moisha asked.

"Well, unlike you, some of us have jobs," she replied with a present attitude that was uncalled for.

Jesus be a fence because this bitch done lost her mind, Moisha thought.

"I have a job that I start in two months," I said, as if she didn't know.

"Well, I've been busy with work. I'll talk to you when I am free," Zara said, then ended the call.

Moisha couldn't help but to feel some type of way due to the type of friendship she and Zara had. Moisha knew there was something wrong with Zara but she didn't have time to kiss her ass to see what was up. She would soon come around when she wanted to. Until then, Moisha was going to do her.

Just as Moisha got up out of bed, her phone began to ring from an unknown number. A look of confusion began to cover her face but nonetheless, she answered her phone.

"Hello?" she said, as she went out onto her balcony in nothing but shorts and a black PINK sports bra.

"Hey, is this Moisha?" a familiar voiced asked.

"This is she and this is..."

"Wesley. We met at-" Wesley rushed to say.

"Oh, I know and I remember." She smiled.

"Hope I didn't call too early," he said.

"Oh, you're fine. It's only eleven," she said.

There was an awkward silence then Wesley spoke up, "So, I was actually calling to see what you were doing tonight and if maybe you would allow me to take you on a date?"

Moisha smirked. She hasn't been on a date before; this would be first. Moisha didn't want to sound so desperate, so she just said, "Sure. Why not?"

Wesley chuckled. "I'll text you the details alright?"

"Alright," she spoke, then he ended the call. "Yay!" Moisha screamed then ran and jumped into her bed, like a little love struck teenager when their crush talks to them.

"I need to find something to wear," she said to herself out loud. Just as she was about to go into her closet, she needed to first know where they were going so she just chilled out for the moment. She placed her phone back on the charger, then hopped into the shower to take care of her hygiene.

***

After getting dressed, Moisha closed her balcony door, then she checked her phone, looking at her plans for later on tonight.

Wesley 12:03 pm

Hey Beautiful, so tonight I figured we would go to this Italian spot downtown, I could pick you up around 7, if that's okay with you?

Moisha 1:23pm

Well, just give me he address and I'll drive myself. Cannot wait!

Moisha pressed send then placed her phone back down. She began to think about what to wear tonight. Just as she was about to get deep in thought, her phone began to ring. It was her mother, so she answered quickly.

"Hey mama," Moisha answered.

"I'm glad you decided to answer. You graduate college and just act as if you do not know me," Faith said, fake acting hurt.

"Ma. It's not that at allllll, but guess what? I have a date tonight!" Moisha rejoiced, as if her mother could see.

"My baby is growing up way too fast. You graduating college, going on dates now, then as soon as I know it, you'll be married and move across the country. I wasn't prepared," she explained.

"Ma…" Moisha laughed. "Just stop it"

"Girl bye, but who is this, this man that will be taking my baby out?" her mother asked.

For the most part, Moisha and her mother had a pretty close relationship. Growing up, her mother wasn't really strict, only when it came to school work. Moisha guess that was a perk of having a younger parent.

"His name is Wesley and to be honest, that's all I know," Moisha spoke truthfully.

"Girl, tell me about him when you know more." Her mother laughed. "Well, that's all I wanted was to check up on you and give you a good laugh. Talk to you later baby, I love you!"

"I love you too ma." The call ended and once again, Moisha put it back on the charger so it could get a full charge. She waltzed into her kitchen, going into the refrigerator to get some leftovers from the night before when she cooked. She put the meatloaf, cornbread, and asparagus into the microwave and set it on the timer for a minute.

The doorbell rang and Moisha definitely wasn't expecting any visitors, so this caught her off guard. She looked through the peephole and saw a man in a work suit standing there with flowers. "The hell," she whispered to herself then opened the door.

"Flowers for Ms. Moisha Jones," he said, giving the two dozen of white roses to Moisha. He left, then she shut the door. She looked at the card.

Have a nice day beautiful –Anonymous

Moisha cracked a smile and placed the flowers on the counter. "How does Wesley know where I live?" she questioned herself while laughing.

***

The clack of her nude heels touching the cement sounded when Moisha stepped out of the car. Moisha did look quite nice. She was dressed exquisitely with her black two piece, which consisted of a black crop top and a much fitted knee length skirt. She sighed as she grabbed her nude clutch, closing her door. She just hoped that this wasn't too much for the occasion. After locking her door, Moisha was on her way into the restaurant. Her stomach turned the moment she stepped foot in the place, she was beyond nervous.

"I'm here for Mr. Wesley-"

"Right over here ma'am." Moisha was guided to a private, excluded room with a table for two. Wesley smiled, getting up once he saw Moisha. He went ahead and gave her a hug then pulled out her seat for her.

"How you doing sweetheart?" he asked, once they were both situated.

Moisha smiled. "Good. I just wanted to say thanks for the roses. They smell so good and they are beautiful. That was sweet of you."

As Moisha rambled about the roses, Wesley was trying to remember whether he got her flowers or not. He didn't even know where she lived. He didn't want to rain on her parade so he said, "You're welcome beautiful."

Wesley hated to tell her that but she seemed all too happy. "So, how was your day?" he asked, changing the subject. He didn't want her saying anything else about the flowers she thought he sent.

"Honestly, this is the highlight of my day," she spoke.

"So, you do not work?" he questioned.

"Well, I just graduated and I start work in the fall," she told him.

"Ah, alright well I work in industrial maintenance," he began explaining. As Wesley went further into his job description, Moisha couldn't help but to look at his features. Soon, the waiter came, snapping her out of her thoughts. They ordered their drinks then Wesley proceeded to talk more, about himself. Moisha was fine with learning about him, but he seemed to be a little conceited.

"So, tell me about you," Wesley said with a smile.

Finally, Moisha thought to herself.

"Well honestly, there is not much to me. Might as well say it. I'll be a Magazine Editor. I'm twenty-three-" Moisha started, but then Wesley cut her off.

"Ahh, when I was twenty-three…" Wesley began to speak and Moisha instantly tuned herself out. He even talked as they ate. Moisha wasn't the type of female to point out flaws and hold a person to it but Moisha didn't know if she and Wesley could move further in their friendship. If he was going to be talking about himself all the time, they couldn't.

"Excuse me while I go use the restroom," Moisha said.

"Alright sweetheart" Wesley said, flashing a smile.

Moisha got up, leaving the private area in search for the restroom. She didn't have to pee but she did need a minute. She went into the women's restroom, looking at herself. She ran her hands over her edges, looking at the neat ninja bun and exhaled. She applied her plump lip gloss by MAC and went ahead out the door.

"I'm so sorry," Moisha said, as she realized she hit someone.

"You fine," a familiar voice said.

Moisha cocker her head back. "Prince?"

"Moisha? What you doing here?" he asked.

"Honestly. A date," she replied, rolling her eyes. Prince tried his best for his facial expression not to match how he felt to hear that.

"Didn't seem so enthused right there," Prince chuckled. He looked down the hall then around. He noticed the janitor's closet. Before he knew it, he slightly grabbed Moisha then went into the janitor's closet, closing the door.

"Prince, what the hell?" Moisha said and he just put his index finger over her mouth, indicating her to be quiet.

"You look nice," she spoke, looking at the outfit he had on.

"Thanks ma," he replied, then stared into her eyes. Moisha looked up into his eyes and was captivated by them. Before she knew it, she felt the touch of his soft, juicy lips. Prince wrapped his hands around Moisha's waist, bringing her in closer to him. Their lips moved in sync and to Prince's surprise, Moisha didn't freak out or some shit.

"Mmmm, Prince!" Moisha said, breaking the kiss. "I am so sorry but I kind of have to go," she said then waved bye. Moisha came out of the janitor's closet and fixed herself, so she could look normal because that kiss knocked Moisha's socks off and she wasn't even wearing any.

"Came back looking more beautiful than when you left," Wesley complimented and Moisha smiled.

Thirty minutes later, Wesley was walking Moisha back to her car. "Thank you for everything Welsey." Moisha smiled, getting into her car.

"It's no problem, call me when you're home," he said and Moisha closed the door.

Wesley began walking to his car and Moisha locked the door, thinking about the kiss she and Prince shared. It captivated her, wanting more, but she knew that it was probably a one-time thing. Moisha began to back up out of her parking spot, going home. She turned the radio on just to hear a song that explained her current situation, somewhat.

I only think of you on two occasions

That's day and night

I'd go for broooooooke if I could be with you

Only you can make it right

An autumn love is special

At this time of the year

But when the leaves are gone

Does that love disappear

I never underestimate the new love of spring

But I'm glad to say in my heart

I know my love's lasting

Moisha rolled her eyes, changing the station, only to hear another song that explained her current situation.

This one is for the boys in the Polos

Entrepreneur niggas & the moguls

He could ball with the crew, he could solo

But I think I like him better when he down low

And I think I like him better with the fitted cap on

He ain't even gotta try to put the mac on

He just gotta give me that look, when he give me that look

Then the panties comin' off, off, uh

Excuse me, you're a hell of a guy you know

I really got a thing for American guys

I mean, sigh, sickenin' eyes

I can tell that you're in touch with your feminine side, oh

Yes I did, yes I did, somebody please tell him who the F I is

I am Nicki Minaj, I mack them dudes up,

back coupes up, and chuck the deuce up

"You know what, I'm listening to some gospel." Moisha then turned to the Gospel radio, listening to that the rest of the way home.

***

Moisha woke up to the ringing of her phone; she turned over and answered. "Hello?" she spoke in her sleepy voice.

"Mo, you said you were going to take me to school today!" Mya screamed into the phone.

Moisha's eyes widened, then she looked at the time. It was seven fifteen and Mya's school started at seven thirty. "Ah, shit. Mya, I'm on my way. Be outside at the mailbox, okay?!"

Mya's car was in the shop, their dad was at work, and their mother had an appointment, so it was up to Moisha to take Mya to school. Moisha totally forgot; she usually would have set an alarm. Moisha quickly got out of bed and ran to the bathroom. She quickly brushed her teeth. She took off her bonnet and her pajamas. She brushed her hair into a ponytail then put on a random t-shirt and sweats. Moisha then slid her feet into her pink Airforce 1's. She grabbed her keys and purse, then headed out the door.

It didn't take her that long to get to her parents' house and just as instructed, Mya was by the mailbox with a mug on her face. "Knock the face off," Moisha said then sped off.

"Can I at least get some breakfast?"

Mya's class started in five minutes; she was already late. "Shit, why not," Moisha said. They stopped by McDonald's then kept going.

"How was your date?" Mya asked.

"How you know?" Moisha said.

"Mommy." Mya smiled.

"I figured and it was okay. I'm still thinking whether or not if I want to keep him around," Moisha spoke truthfully.

Moisha pulled up curb side to Mya's school and Mya began getting up. "Well, think of it like this. If you have to think about whether or not you want to keep around, then just don't." Mya laughed, then closed the door. Moisha told her bye and pulled off. She couldn't deny the fact that Mya was right. Wow.

Moisha was out, so she figured she would run a few errands before it got too late in the day. Moisha was troubled about the fact that she didn't have any way to get in contact with Prince. It was like he controlled when they saw each other. Moisha wondered if he'd be at *Heaven's Kitchen*, just by chance.

She figured, after her errands, she would go by there and pick something up. After going to the back and taking some shoes back to Macy's, Moisha made her way over to the soul food place.

She pulled up and smiled. Prince was outside talking to some man. He turned around and smirked because he knew Moisha's car. He said something to the man then walked over to Moisha. "So, is my place responsible for your thighs?" he asked.

Moisha laughed and said, "Maybe," then got out the car.

"Please, do not look at me. I look like shit right now," Moisha complained.

"Whatever." Prince laughed.

"I'mma go ahead and get my food. I'll be back out," Moisha said, then began walking towards the door.

"Tell him I got you!" he called.

She replied, "Thank you" over her shoulder then went into the place.

Prince walked back up to his good friend Brandon. "That's you fam? She got a fat ass," Brandon commented, looking at Moisha through the window.

"Watch ya' mouth bruh and it will be in a good month," Prince said confidently.

"What makes you say that?" Brandon asked.

"Because she needs a good nigga that can treat her right and I'm that nigga," Prince chuckled.

"Shit, shoot ya' shot fam," he said.

Prince laughed, "Like Jordan in the 4th." Both Prince and Brandon shared a good laugh. As they were laughing, Moisha walked out the restaurant with her food in a bag.

"What you get?" Prince questioned.

"Uh. Cornbread, chicken dumpling, chicken lasagna," she replied. Prince smiled because chicken lasagna was actually one of his favorite things his mother cooked. "Yeah. It is my favorite. I like regular lasagna but it's something about that chicken," Moisha said.

"Oh, let me introduce you," Prince said, looking over to Brandon. Moisha smiled. "This is my good friend Brandon. He is actually one of my business partners. We're thinking about opening a club," he explained.

"Nice to meet you-" Moisha cut her sentence short when she noticed Zara getting out her car. "I'm so sorry. I'll be right back," Moisha apologized.

"Zara!" she called out. Her back was turned and she was about to get back into the car.

"Fuck! What Moisha!?" Zara yelled. Zara turned around and Moisha saw the problem. It was nothing to be ashamed of at all or any reason to isolate yourself. Zara was pregnant and it was obvious.

"Why you didn't tell me? You my bitch Za' and you hiding shit. Come on girl, our friendship is not like this at all," Moisha said.

Zara began to sniff. "Just uh. Let me get my food and come back to my place."

Moisha nodded. "Alright" Moisha walked back over to Prince and Brandon. Prince had a confused look on his face. He, of course, remembered Zara. "My name is Moisha, sorry once again," she explained.

"You good; the pleasure is all mines," Brandon replied with a smile.

"Anyways!" Prince interjected. "What you plan on doing today?" he asked, as they both began walking towards Moisha's car.

"Go over Zara's then just chill. I had to take my sister to school and I forgot, which is why I'm dressed like this," Moisha said, looking down at the clothing she had on.

"You fine. I believe you look good in anything," Prince said, admiring Moisha.

Moisha had chocolate skin, a great figure, and a pretty face; Prince couldn't help but be attracted to her.

"Thank you, that's sweet of you say." Moisha blushed, trying to hide it. Prince watched her as she blushed. She tried to hide it but was very unsuccessful.

"I do not have your number because?" Moisha asked because she thought that usually the man would ask by now.

"Because you never asked." Prince smirked.

"You ain't ask for mines though," Moisha challenged.

"Trust me, if I wanted to get in contact with you, I can," Prince spoke.

Moisha nodded. "Wow, well put your number in my phone and I'll hit you up later," Moisha said, giving him her rose gold iPhone 6s.

Prince put his number in her phone then gave it back. "How about tonight?" he asked her.

"Alright then, tonight," Moisha replied. She saw Zara getting into her car, so she figured it was about time for her to depart.

"Aight, talk to you later ma," Prince spoke. They shared a quick embrace and Moisha got into her car, going towards Zara's place.

***

Zara and Moisha sat eating and talking on Zara's couch. Moisha felt as if they needed to have this talk anyway.

"My body was changing and the signs were there. I... I do not know. I guess I ignored them. Then I went ahead and took a test and here I am," Zara said, shrugging.

"But the fact that you snapped on me that day. It low-key hurt," Moisha spoke, telling the truth.

"I was just frustrated and wanted to be alone. I didn't mean to take out my frustration on you, girl. I hope you can forgive me, honestly," Zara apologized.

"Of course, now when you due boo?" Moisha asked Zara.

"In February, I'm pretty excited," Zara rejoiced. "Even with EJ being absent," Zara said.

"Wow, the fact that we do not have no idea where that nigga at," Moisha said in disbelief.

"Mo, I think he's dead to be honest but then again, that's just wishful thinking," Zara replied.

Moisha laughed a little bit then picked up the phone. "Wait missy. What's going on with you and the kidnapper?" Zara asked.

"He is not a kidnapper," Moisha said in his defense.

"Mhmmmm," Zara said with her 'bitch bye' face.

"Anyways, I mean. I am kind of feeling him. I just do not know him well enough," Moish replied.

"I think he's feeling you too," Zara said.

"And how do you know?" Moisha asked.

"Bitch, it's obvious as hell!" Zara yelled, throwing a pillow at Moisha for being so dumb.

Moisha dodged the pillow, laughing. "I mean, I'm just going to see how everything plays out."

"You go bitch, get you a man." Zara smiled.

Moisha smiled. "But I'll wait for him to get me because I'm not trying to get a man that doesn't want to be got," Moisha preached.

Zara began clapping and then waving her hand as if she was in church. "Yas bitch! I feel the spurit" she then said, resulting in the both of them laughing. Moisha's phone began to vibrate with a text from Wesley.

Hello beautiful!

"Who texting us?" Zara asked, peeking over Moisha's shoulder.

"Wesley," Moisha groaned.

"Do not let him go too soon, we need options." Zara cheesed.

"Mmm. If you say so," Moisha replied.

Chapter Four

Moisha was up early this Wednesday morning at the gym. It was eight in the morning and she was trying to get in shape. As she was walking on the treadmill, she could feel some of the stares of the men. They didn't faze her at all because she came to the gym to work out and to only work out. Moisha turned up the speed of the treadmill a little and it was now at a jog. She had Chief Keef blasting in her ear, which was keeping her hyped.

After another thirty minutes, Moisha was done and ready to go. She grabbed her things off the treadmill then proceeded into the locker room. She went to her designated locker, putting the code in. It opened and she grabbed her bag. She wiped the sweat off herself, then put the towel into the bag.

Moisha was on her way out when she noticed Wesley walking out as well. Moisha flashed a fake smile as Wesley began walking over to her.

"I didn't know you worked out," he spoke with a smile. He tried to hug her but Moisha stopped him.

"I do not smell very pleasant," Moisha said.

"Alright sweetheart," he said.

"But yeah, I'm trying to shed a few pounds," Moisha explained. Wesley looked at the spandex and sports bra Moisha wore. She looked fine to him.

"I mean, if you want to then sure, but I feel like you do not need to. You're perfectly fine the way you are," Wesley spoke. In his eyes, Moisha was perfect.

"Awh, thank you Wesley. That was sweet of you." Moisha smiled. "Well, I have to get going. It was good seeing you," Moisha then said.

"It was good seeing you also," he replied, licking his lips as he got a view of Moisha from the back. Moisha got into her car going back home, so she was able to freshen up.

***

Prince was talking to his team; something needed to be done fast. EJ got Prince out of about ten thousand dollars and Prince wanted his money, which is why they did the whole operation of raiding EJ's house. EJ just vanished and Prince was going to find that nigga, whether he was dead or alive.

"So, I need everyone to go a hunid' and ten percent. I want that nigga's head. Any traces of where he might be, report that to Lonzo," Prince explained.

"Everyone good? Oh yeah, whoever finds EJ's dumb ass dead or alive, that's an extra five stacks added on to your pay. Do I need to touch on anything else?"

"No," various men said and Prince nodded his head.

"Can someone get me the sell report for this month? Thanks, y'all good," he said and he left.

Prince went into another room that was only accessible by key. That room was where the safe was. He went into the room, then into a closet that was locked by a pin pad. He input the code then opened the closet up. He bent down and inputted the code in the safe. The safe opened up and millions, yes, millions were in Prince's eyes but there were multiple things that had to be paid for and priorities come first. Prince got out the black duffle bag, putting exactly one million in there. He shut the safe and proceeded on his way out the closet and out the room. He made sure everything was locked before he departed. Prince headed straight out the place and to the bank, where he was able to put about two thousand in to go towards bills.

Prince always thought about getting an assistant but it was hard trusting anyone. So, he just did shit himself. Prince was really good at keeping business and personal issues separate. So, no one really knew about Prince unless he told you. He liked it like that and it was going to remain that way.

Prince wanted Moisha and he was going to get her. It was that simple. He just hoped she wanted him back. Moisha was definitely a different type of female and Prince saw that. He really wanted to show her what a real nigga was and what he had to offer. Niggas fuck up when they feel as if they girl not going anywhere, so they do what they want. Best believe that shit that Prince did to get Moisha; he would continue it and do even more.

Prince was done running all around Memphis doing errands. He wanted to do a pop-up at Moisha's place but he figured that would be rude as fuck, so he just simply called.

"Hello?" she answered.

"Hey, how you doing?" he asked, turning the radio down.

"Good, how about you, Prince?" she asked in return.

"I'm good, out hustlin' making that dolla'. What you up to today? You have time for me?" He smirked.

"The question is do you have time for me?" Moisha asked.

Prince chuckled. "I always have time for you ma', you can b'lieve that," he replied. He could tell Moisha was blushing; the phone was silent.

"Well, I have a whole day to myself and I do not have a thing planned," Moisha explained,

"So, you trying to spend the rest of the day with me?" he asked.

"Shit. Why not?"

***

Prince told Moisha he would pick her up from her house; she gave him the address and he then proceeded. Once Moisha was in the car, Prince teased, "You just cannot get away from me, can you?"

Moisha laughed, not entertaining him. It seemed as if every time Moisha was around Prince, she was smiling. Prince began driving and Moisha didn't have no clue where to. She then noticed them pulling up to a gated community. Once the gate sensed Prince's car, it opened. Prince waved to the gate keeper then proceeded to his house. Moisha looked out the window as they road through the luxurious neighborhood. There were houses of all different shapes and sizes, but nonetheless, Moisha was amazed. It was a very well kept neighborhood. They turned down a street from the main road and after about three houses down, they pulled into a driveway.

"This is your house?" Moisha asked.

Prince nodded. "It was just a little something for myself, but once I get a family or whatever, I'll probably get something bigger," he explained.

"This seems big enough for a family though," Moisha said.

"I wan't 'bout seven or eight kids; this is only a three bedroom. Come on," he said after parking into the garage. He and Moisha got out the car. Moisha could see his other car was an all-black Porsche Boxster. It was pretty nice. Black seemed to be the choice of color for his cars.

Moisha followed Prince into his home. Prince took his shoes off by the door, so Moisha did the same. It was beautiful on the inside as well. "You look like you have expensive taste," Moisha said, as they walked through his kitchen. Everything seemed to be over the top.

"Thanks to my mother; she picked everything out but I do have expensive taste," he replied.

"Well, when you have the money to buy expensive things; why not have expensive taste," Moisha said and they both laughed.

"Let me give you a little tour," he said and Moisha began following him. From the kitchen, they walked through the foyer then into a hall ways.

"So, my office is right here," he said, opening the door. "This is where I am majority of the time when I'm home and here's my at home gym," he said, then opened that door. Moisha was surprised because it looked exactly like a little gym.

"Onto upstairs now," Prince instructed.

They went back out to the foyer and then up the main steps. Prince had two guest bedrooms and then his room. He opened the double doors and then began walking in.

His room was black and gold, the walls were gold with white crowning, and his furniture was black. His room even accompanied a balcony. "My closet," Prince said, as he opened his closet door. It was, of course, a walk-in closet and it was big as hell. Everything was neat. "You have to have a maid," Moisha said.

Prince nodded. "Yeah. She comes twice a week," he replied. They went into his bathroom and that was it. Moisha had seen enough.

"Wow. Your home is immaculate," Moisha complimented.

"Thank you," he replied with a smile.

"My little condo doesn't even compare." She laughed.

"I bet it's nice though," he said.

Moisha nodded, it was nice. She loved her little condo. "You hungry?" Prince asked her.

"Yeah, I could go for some food," Moisha replied, as they began walking out of Prince's room.

"Good, because I am. I was going to cook," Prince said, they were now downstairs in the kitchen.

Moisha sat in one of the chairs in the island. "Let me find out you know your way around the kitchen," Moisha said, as she watched him wash his hands and get a pot out. To make it even better, he was doing all this while being shirtless. Moisha could tell he worked out by his body. He was very well fit.

"I know my way around a lot of things," Prince said, smirking.

As Prince cooked, they engaged in small talk, like where they see themselves in five years. Moisha saw herself well into her career or maybe getting her master's degree. Of course, it would be good to be working her way towards having a family or at least in a relationship. With Prince, it was the same and, of course, making billions.

"So, why you single?" Prince asked Moisha.

"To be honest, I do not even know. I do not know if it's because I'm unattractive-"

"I do not want you to even say no shit like that," Prince spat.

Moisha exhaled. "I just do not like men necessarily looking at me and maybe because I'm not out here dressing half naked and going out to the hottest clubs. You know, shit like that," Moisha explained. "So, why are you single?" Moisha asked Prince. He seemed like the perfect man.

"It's just hard trying to find something real. A lot of the females I encountered were money hungry, always looking to get, and didn't want to give. It was just hard to find someone to love you for you and not what you got," he explained.

"Wow… that's crazy because you seem, so… so perfect," Moisha admitted.

"No. You're perfect," Prince spoke.

Moisha smiled, then got quiet. Was she developing feelings for Prince? It hadn't even been that long. Yeah, she was feeling him, but now it was on something serious.

"Aight, I'm done," Prince said. He sat a plate in front of Moisha. "Ribs, with my special BBQ sauce, cornbread, and sweet potato casserole."

"Damn, that was fast" Moisha said, as her mouth watered by just looking at the food.

"Well, we've been talking for like an hour or two. Can I call you Mo?" Prince asked.

"Sure, everyone else does," Moisha said and began eating.

"You are a really good cook. Just not better than me," Moisha said.

"Oh okay. So, I guess you going to cook me something one day, so we can see," he said, as he too began eating.

"You got it." Moisha smiled.

After they ate, Moisha said she would get the dishes. Prince, of course, helped her. "It feels really good having you around," Prince said.

In return, Moisha flicked some water on you. "Oh yeah, you done fucked up," Prince said but before he could do anything, Moisha took off running. Prince immediately ran after her. Moisha got upstairs. Just as she was about to go into one of the guest bedrooms, he snatched her and brought her into him. She couldn't help but to laugh; she wiped the water off his face still laughing. Prince picked Moisha up then took her to his room, where he laid her on the bed.

"Let me find out you strong." Moisha smiled, mesmerized by his body. Prince had damn near an eight pack. Prince and Moisha shared a quick kiss.

"Mo', I'm going to be honest. I want you to be mine, but I do not want us to rush into anything," Prince said, cutting out the bullshit.

"Damn…um, well, how about we just take things slow," Moisha said.

***

The moment Moisha said she wanted to take things slow with Prince was the point her life somewhat changed. Prince was nothing but a gentleman, sweet and compassionate. They were always together, just them, to the point where Moisha was ignoring the other people in her life. It wasn't on purpose at all. Moisha was just happy; she was working on something good with a good man. Weeks passed by and Moisha found herself falling hard for Prince, but that wasn't bad because he felt the same way.

"Hello?" Moisha said. She had just woke up and surprisingly, she was home.

"Wow, bitch you finally answered," Zara said with a laugh.

Moisha rolled her eyes, as if Zara could see her. "Whatever, what's up?" Moisha said, fully getting up. She went into the bathroom then put her phone on speaker.

"Um, I guess you forgot what you were supposed to be doing today?" Zara said.

"Shit if I know," Moisha said, waiting for Zara to go ahead and say it.

"Doctors," Zara mentioned.

"Damnnnn! I'm supposed to go with you to your appointment today. I still have time, just let me get ready," Moisha explained.

"Alright Mo, I'm about to be headed out the door."

"I'll see you at the doctor's office boo," Moisha said and Zara went ahead and hung up. Moisha placed her phone down, undressed, and got into the shower. After the shower, she took care of the rest of her hygiene then began getting dressed.

Moisha dressed in lightwash denim jeans, a nice white button up Ralph Lauren shirt that was short sleeved, and her rainbow flips flops. Since she was in such a hurry, she just slicked down her edges and put her hair into a sloppy ninja bun.

She put some clear lip gloss on and sprayed some Ed Hardy perfume on, then kept it moving. Moisha made her way to her car then made her way towards the doctor's office. As she was driving, her phone began to ring. She grabbed it, answering as she remained focused on her driving.

"Hello."

"Hey baby girl, how you doing this morning?" Prince asked.

Moisha smiled. "I'm good. I'm on the way to Zara's appointment. What about you?"

"I'm about to start packing actually," Prince said.

Moisha scrunched up her face in confusion. "Packing for why?" Moisha asked.

"I have to go to Nashville to talk about this space I'm trying to buy for my club," Prince explained.

"So, have long you going to be gone?" Moisha asked, as she pulled into the parking lot.

"Three or four days… I won't be gone for too long Mo," he said, reassuring Moisha.

"Alright, well I'm about to go into the doctor's office, talk to you later."

"Alright baby girl," he replied and ended the call. Moisha put her phone in her purse, then exited her car and locked the doors.

Once Moisha got inside the building, she spotted Zara sitting down on her phone.

"Za'," Moisha said, sitting down beside her.

Zara looked up with a sad face, like she was not feeling good or something. "You alright?" Moisha asked, as she crossed her legs.

"Girl, this morning I was throwing up and shit. I just want to go to sleep all day, which I will do after I come from this appointment. Wait, no we need to get some food first," Zara explained. After that, she was called by a nurse.

Both Zara and Moisha got up and followed the nurse to a room. The nurse introduced herself then Zara introduced Moisha.

"Is the father coming today?" the nurse asked,

"Probably not. Probably not ever, to be quite honest," Zara replied and Moisha's eyes widened. Zara saw Moisha's look. "What? It's the truth," she said and the nurse left to go get the doctor.

It took about ten minutes for Zara's doctor to come in. "Hey Zara." She smiled.

"Hey and look, I brought my best friend Moisha," Zara pointed out.

Moisha smiled and the doctor then introduced herself. "So, let's go ahead and get into it. Zara, lay back for me hun and lift your shirt up." Zara wasn't big at all, but she was showing. Zara was about seven weeks.

After about thirty minutes, the two got Zara's ultrasound picture and left. "We going to eat right?" Zara asked, as they were walking outside.

Moisha nodded. "Yeah but where you want to go?" Moisha asked, but she already knew the answer.

"Heaven's." Zara smiled, then got into her car. Moisha nodded then went to her car.

Moments later, the duet was at Heaven's eating in. They decided to go ahead and have some girl talk. Moisha needed to get Zara caught up. Moisha sipped her lemonade. "Well, what you want to know?" she asked.

Zara was eating her chicken wings. "Well, have you gave up the punani yet?" Zara asked, lowering her voice.

"No," Moisha said.

"Am I supposed to?" she asked.

"I mean, well… you do not want him going to other women when you can give it to him," Zara said matter-of-factly.

Moisha's face softened. "Well, he and I aren't together though," Moisha replied.

"So, what are y'all doing?" Zara asked with a face of confusion.

"I mean, we're taking things slow, still learning each other but I do not think Prince will do anything like that. He do not seem like the type to bullshit with me," Moisha explained.

"Remember, like you said, y'all still learning each other so you never know," Zara said and Moisha began to think on it. Her mind was wandering, all because of Zara.

"See, now you thinking. Girl, do not let these niggas bullshit you," Zara said with a wink.

***

That night, Moisha had got ready for bed then Facetimed Prince.

"I was waiting on you to hit me up," Prince said, once he answered. It was pretty evident that he was in a hotel.

"You could've called anytime or text, you know," Moisha said, thinking about what Zara said earlier at *Heaven's*. There was silence for about two minutes and Prince ain't like it.

"What's wrong Mo'?" he asked Moisha; something seemed to be troubling her.

"I know we not together but would you bullshit me?" Moisha asked.

"Bullshit you? Have I done anything or said anything that would make you even ask me that huh?" he said, raising his voice a little.

"No," Moisha replied.

"Then why ask me Mo'?" he asked and Moisha got quiet. "You must've been talking to someone and they filled your head up with bullshit. Look, I'm going to say this and then talk to you later. Do not let no one talk you into fucking up something good," he said.

"You right," Moisha said.

Oh, I know," Prince said confidently. "Now, good night baby girl," he said, then ended the call. Moisha didn't want Prince mad at her, so from this point on, she wasn't going to listen to anyone else. But, she wanted to talk to him for longer, not for that little ten minutes.

Chapter Five

A Week later...

Today was Monday, it was a new week, and exactly two weeks until Moisha started her job as an editor. Today, she had to attend orientation. At the orientation, she basically was going to be given information about the magazine, what was expected from her, how she should dress, and other helpful information. The orientation started at ten, so Moisha woke up at eight and began taking care of her hygiene.

Prince was, of course, back in Memphis. He had been very busy and hadn't really seen Moisha. He, of course, kept in contact.

Once Moisha was out of the shower, she began brushing her teeth and then washing her face. Her phone began to ring and to her luck, it was Prince. She happily answered. "Hello?"

"Hey, I'm at your door, open up," he said and Moisha walked out of her bathroom and to the door. She opened it and there stood Prince. The moment he came in the house, he closed the door and hugged Moisha. "I missed you."

"I missed you too. I was getting ready, you know I have orientation today," Moisha said, going back into her room with Prince right behind her. Prince laid on Moisha's bed as she was in the bathroom putting on lotion. After she took her hair out her bonnet, she brushed it then began flat ironing it. Earlier this year, Moisha had gotten a sew-in and truth be told, she missed it. She probably would get one before she started her job.

"Oh shit, I ain't know you was there," Moisha said as she noticed Prince in the doorway.

He smirked. "You cute," he teased. "What you wearing?" he then asked.

"This peach pantsuit and nude pumps," she replied. "It's laid out on the window seat," Moisha informed.

Prince went over to the window seat, seen what she was wearing, and nodded his head, knowing Moisha was going to look beautiful in the outfit.

Prince went out of Moisha's room and she took that as a chance to put on her undergarments. After putting on a black bra and matching lace panties, she began putting on her outfit. Prince came back to a fully dressed Moisha.

Just as Moisha was going back to the bathroom, he stopped her by grabbing her hand. "Slow down," he chuckled. "You running around like a chicken with its head cut off," he added. "Come here…relaxxxxx," he suggested. Moisha stood in between Prince's legs while he stared at her.

Moisha bent down and gave him a kiss. Their kiss deepened, involving tongue, and Prince found his way to Moisha's ass, slapping it and grabbing it. "Owwww!" Moisha screamed.

Prince cheesed and Moisha groaned. She then looked at the time and it was going on nine o'clock. "I'm going to have to leave soon," Moisha warned.

"After your orientation, what you have to do?"

"Nothing. I was probably going to hang out with my little sister when she got out school."

"Oh alright," Prince replied.

"We can come by your house. You plan on being home?" she asked.

He nodded. "Yeah, I plan on being home for the rest of the day," he reassured.

***

Moisha just got to the building with thirty minutes to spare. It wasn't far from her house at all, about a ten minute drive with no traffic. She grabbed her purse, then got out her car. After locking her door, she began going towards the building. Once inside, she went up to the receptionist.

"How may I help you?" she asked with an obviously fake smile, but Moisha paid it no mind.

"I'm here for the orientation," Moisha replied.

"You're going to go down the hall then to the right," she instructed.

"Thank you," Moisha replied, then went as directed. She came upon the room, which was the size of a ballroom. First, she had to pick up the name tag with her name and employee number, so she could be identified. There were about 10 or 15 other people already seated, ready to start the seminar part of the orientation. Moisha knew this was about to be a long day.

After a quick information session, thirty minutes later, they were spilt into groups based on job position. Each type of job had a designated floor. Moisha's group was taken up to the 2nd floor, the editing floor. It was only five people in her group, which made it very easy. Everyone was designated to a cubicle and was told what their starting salary was. They were told how many articles they were to edit a week. Each week, you had a set number you had to edit. Moisha was ready, she was exited.

By twelve, they were done. Moisha decided she was going to go by her parents' house then wait until Mya got out of school to go get her, then go over Prince's house.

"Is that my oldest baby girl?" Mar asked. Moisha smiled, closing the door.

"Daddy, you decided to be home for once," Moisha teased, going into the living room to see her father drinking a beer.

"Have you heard from your brother?" he asked her.

Moisha shook her head. "No. You know Mathew is in his own little world but anyways, I had my job orientation today!" Moisha rejoiced.

"How did it go?"

"Great, I'm ready." She cheesed.

"That's good, I'm proud of you baby girl," he said. "So, what you been doing?" he then added.

"I've been really just hanging with Zara, helping her out with her situation you know," she explained.

"Well, that's good. Tell if she needs anything from me or your mother, we got her. She's like family, so we do not mind helping her either," he said to Moisha's surprise. Moisha looked down at the time and it was about time for Mya to get out school.

"Well, I have to get going daddy; your daughter is staying with me for the rest of the day."

"Alright and oh lord, y'all be good!" he said.

"Bye, I love you," Moisha said over her shoulder.

"I love you too Mo'," he replied and Moisha shut the door, going to her car.

She made her way over to Mya's high school and it was so much commotion. Moisha had to get in line with the other cars to get to the front of the school. As she waited, she sent Mya a quick message, letting her know that she was out front. Within ten minutes, Mya was getting into the car.

"Awh, so you really do love me?" Mya said, once she got into the car.

"Why you say that?" Moisha asked, going into the direction of Prince's house.

"Because I didn't have to ask you, you just popped up," Mya explained. "So, where we going? Because my house or even your house is the other way. Better not be kidnapping me," Mya said, looking out the window.

"Girl. We're going my friend's house," Moisha said and Mya plugged her phone up into the AUX.

You used to call me on my, you used to, you used to

You used to call me on my cell phone

Late night when you need my love

Call me on my cell phone

Late night when you need my love

I know when that hotline bling

That can only mean one thing

I know when that hotline bling

Drake's *Hotline Bling* was playing and Mya was singing along. That was when Moisha knew this was going to be a long ride. They pulled up to the gate and Moisha put in the code. "Oh shit now," Mya said, scoping the place. The gate opened and they drove right on in. "Is this where millionaires live Mo'?" Mya asked her big sister.

"Probably," Moisha said. They arrived at Prince's house and Mya couldn't keep her mouth shut. "Mya, just be chill."

"How? Girl, this big ass house and you want me to be chill. This like three of my houses and about fifty of your condo," Mya said, then began to laugh.

Moisha shot her a stare. "Shut up and come on." Moisha got out the key that Prince let her get. She only went to his house, of course, when he was there. She didn't want to intrude on his space too much.

"Prince," Moisha said, as they got inside.

"Wow," Mya said, looking all around.

"Office," was all Prince replied and they went into the direction of the office.

"Hey," Moisha said, as they entered his office.

"Hey Mya, you remember me?" Prince asked her.

"Yeah, I do. Your house is really nice," Mya complimented.

"Thanks lil mama. If y'all want something, I was on the grill earlier and made burgers and hotdogs. Y'all can have some if you want," Prince said.

"Yes and I'm hungry," Mya said and exited the office.

"But you do not even know where the kitchen is," Moisha complained.

"I'll find it!" Mya replied. Prince laughed. "Please do not mind her."

"Mhm, ya' twin," he said. Prince stared at Moisha; she still had on her orientation clothes and wanted to change.

"I guess…" Moisha trailed out. Prince got up out his office chair, going over to Moisha, and he gave her a kiss. He wrapped his arms around her waist, putting his head in her neck. After he gave her neck a few pecks, she went to go change. As Moisha was changing, he took that as the chance to get to know Mya. He went into the kitchen where Mya was for sure stuffing her face.

"I see right now you and your sister like to eat," Prince said with a smirk.

Mya shrugged, smiling. "Yeah, we do."

They both began to laugh and Prince began to make small talk. "So, how old are you, Mya?"

"I'm sixteen, my favorite color is green because I like money. I'm a junior in high school. Well, I'm a sophomore right now but in like a month, I'll be a junior. I go to East Park High, it's year round…." she started.

Damn, Prince thought. He knew from that that Mya like to talk.

"Well then…" Prince said, chuckling.

"I felt like you were going to ask a lot, so I just went ahead and gave it all," she replied.

"Well, I guess nothing ain't wrong with that," Prince replied, getting a burger for himself.

Moisha changed into one of Prince's grey t-shirts and some Nike leggings, then made her way downstairs.

Moisha came back down and she could tell Mya was talking too much. "I know she was talking your head off," Moisha said.

"She's fine," Prince chuckled.

"Yeah, Mo' fall bizack," Mya said, laughing.

"Well, Mya, you can make yourself at home definitely," Prince said.

"Awh, thank you," Mya replied. "I like him. He's nice," she then added. Mya's phone began to ring and she answered and went into another room, so they couldn't hear her.

"How long are y'all staying over here?" Prince asked.

"Probably until Mya wants to leave since this is a school night."

***

Zara was at home about to doze off to sleep when the phone began to ring from an unknown number. She rolled her eyes answering, "Whaaaaat?"

"Zara, it's me baby." Zara quickly sat up.

"EJ?!" she asked in disbelief.

"Yes baby, can you do me a favor?" he asked.

"Like what? You not even trying to see how I am doing, come on EJ…" Zara said.

EJ groaned. "How are you, Zara?"

"I'm alright, you know I am carrying your child. If you care or not," she said with an attitude.

"Why didn't you get an abortion Z?!" he asked.

Zara scrunched up his face. "Really EJ?! Your own child. It's not my fault you want to be a hothead ripping and running the streets. I want my child, therefore, I'm keeping my baby."

"Look baby, I'm sorry, it's just the life that I live. You know I'm not around much and bringing a child into it would be a lot," he explained.

The whole time he was explaining bullshit, Zara had tears streaming down her eyes. It was evident as hell how no good EJ was but sadly, Zara still loved him.

Zara wiped her face. "Whatever EJ, you are selfish!" she spat.

"So, are you going to help a nigga out or what and look, do not be telling Moisha. I'm a little iffy about her."

"Why? That's my best friend," Zara argued.

"What I say?! Anyways, I'm out here in Rossville, I'll text you this address. Just hurry," he instructed, then hung up the phone. Zara placed her phone down then got up. She just put on some sweats, then grabbed her purse and keys. It was about nine at night and Zara was tired but she figured it was her duty. Rossville was about thirty minutes out, so it wasn't going to be a long drive.

About ten minutes later, Zara was out her apartment, going to get EJ. Zara, of course, loved him but she wasn't in love with him as she use to be. EJ got caught up in the wrong things. Zara thinks it's her fault because she knew who she was dealing with before they got together.

As she was driving, her phone began to ring. It was Moisha and she ignored it. Zara had the address EJ gave her set in her phone's GPS and she was in route.

About twenty-five minutes later, she pulled up to a CITGO gas station. She pulled in a parking spot then cut her car off. She exhaled then looked at the time. All she knew was that EJ needed to hurry his ass. Just as she cut the radio down, she saw EJ walking up to her car. She unlocked the door and he got in.

Zara was a nosey type of bitch, so EJ should of known the questions were about to pour in. "So, what you doing out here?" Zara asked.

"Look, I'll explain later. Can you just drive back to yo' place?" he griped.

Zara smacked her teeth and began driving, not saying a word. They were about fifteen minutes away from Memphis when Zara couldn't hold her tongue in anymore.

"I'm tired of making it seem as if we have a good relationship EJ; you treat me basically like shit," Zara said.

She sniffed, trying not to let the tears escape her eyes. EJ really wasn't trying to hear this shit but he just kept quiet. "You just use me, like do you even love me?" she asked.

"I mean… yeah," he replied, not really caring about the subject.

"Then why you just leave me in yo' house like that. Like that really showed me how much you really cared," she said, busting out in tears.

"Baby…look, if those niggas would have saw, they probably would have killed me on sight. I mean you fine," he said.

"But that's not even the point EJ! Ugh. You never get shit. Oh yeah, and the fact that I am bearing your child and you seem to not even give a shit!" she screamed, turning down her street. "Like, do you even plan on being an active father huh?"

"Just chill out," EJ said calmly.

Zara just hushed up as they pulled up to her apartment building. She got out furious and EJ got out as if Zara wasn't just fussing him out. Zara locked the door then went up to her apartment. Both she and EJ went in, and he closed the door. Zara just wanted to go to sleep; she had work at nine-thirty in the morning and it was going on eleven. Zara got back in bed and EJ got in beside her.

"Baby… I'm horny," EJ bugged, as Zara was trying to go to sleep.

"Leave me the hell alone, EJ," Zara said, slapping his hand away from her.

He groaned then got up. "I'll be back."

"Whatever," she griped, then went on to sleep.

The next morning, Zara woke up to see EJ up watching TV. "What time is it?" she asked.

"Just about eight," he replied.   She got up, stretching out.

"So, tell me how you get in the predicament you're in now?" Zara asked, sitting back on the bed.

He exhaled. "Well, I'm going to put it like this. A big time kingpin is out to get me and I want to get him before he gets me," EJ explained.

"Who is this 'kingpin' person?" Zara asked. She was a little curious.

"Prince. He is powerful as hell. I know for a fact he has people out looking for me just because he is just that nigga."

"Moisha… never mind," Zara quickly said. She thought for a second that the Prince he was talking about was Moisha's Prince but Moisha doesn't mess with drug dealers or kingpins or anyone of that caliber.

"Moisha what?" EJ asked.

"Nothing," Zara said.

EJ nodded. "So, what happened when my shit got raided?" EJ asked.

Zara had to think because she couldn't honestly remember anything. "To be honest, I forgot," Zara said, being honest.

"Figures. Can I hide out here for about a month or two?" EJ asked.

"You know you always have a home with me," Zara spoke.

"Thanks ma… don't know what I'd do without you," EJ said.

Zara slightly rolled her eyes then went into the bathroom to get in the shower. Zara just hoped that the Prince that EJ was talking about wasn't Moisha's Prince or else, this wasn't going to end pretty.

Chapter Six

Two Weeks Later…

You see dat outfit bitch

I'm killin you hoes

Cute face and ass swoll

I'm killin you hoes

I got the best pussy out

I'm killin you hoes

And ain't non you can do about

I'm killin you hoes

Trina's *Killin You Hoes* was playing as Moisha was getting ready for her date with Prince. Moisha wore a v-neck sleeveless Khaki fringe dress, along with burgundy fringe heels. The dress and shoes complimented each other very well. Moisha applied a little makeup to her face: foundation, concealer, and mascara. She slayed her eyebrows and put on burgundy lipstick by MAC.

Moisha had got a sew-in about two days ago and she felt so much like herself. She got 22 inches of raw Indian virgin hair sewed in and she was loving it. She put a couple curls here and there then curled her bang; it came out flawless and she felt pretty. Moisha sprayed on some Chanel No.5 perfume, grabbed her clutch, and headed out the door.

Prince texted Moisha, letting her know he was outside. She cheesed then went his way. Moisha saw his

Range then went to the passenger side and got in. "Hey." Moisha smiled then put her seat belt on.

"Answer this for me," Prince said aggressively. "Why you so beautiful? And I'm a need for you to not behind over tonight." He laughed.

Moisha laughed then went on her phone to upload the pictures she took on Instagram and Facebook. Prince's right hand moved from the steering wheel to Moisha's thigh. He slightly rubbed her thigh in an up and down motion. He slightly went to her inner thigh and felt Moisha slightly jump.

"So, that's it?" Prince looked to Moisha smirking.

"No, it's not," Moisha lied.

Prince tried to touch her inner thigh and she didn't let him. "Lie again," he said with a smirk. They were going to downtown Memphis by the Riverwalk. Prince decided to take Moisha to this very exquisite restaurant right on the river. Prince pulled up to the valet service, handing the man his keys and getting the necessary ticket from the man. Prince opened Moisha's door and she got out, taking Prince's hand. Together, they went into the restaurant.

"Reservations for Walker," Prince said.

Moisha made a mental note that 'Walker' was Prince's last name. The hostess led the two all the way outside, right by the river to a secluded area. There was soft music playing and water light reflecting from the water. It was a very beautiful scenery.

Prince got out Moisha's chair and she smiled as she sat down. "Prince, this is so beautiful and peaceful," Moisha mentioned, once Prince got situated.

"It is," he replied back, then began looking at the menu.

Prince and Moisha both ordered wine and were just sipping on that until there food came.

"Soon Moisha, I want to officially make you mines. I know we may not have known each other for very long but I can see us having something that could last forever. Long as you stay the woman that you are, I do not see why not," Prince chuckled. Moisha couldn't help but to blush. "I just want to cater to you tonight."

Damn, this man is heaven sent, Moisha thought to herself.

Their food came and they both began eating, "Oh yeah, and I'm kind of leaving tomorrow," Price said.

Moisha groaned, "Awh"

"Yea, have to go to Nashville. Baby, this is going to be big. Really big," he said. Moisha could tell she was excited. Shit, she was excited for him.

"Well, I'm happy for you," Moisha said.

Their date was coming to an end and Moisha kind of didn't want to leave. It was just the perfect haven. Prince paid and they were on their way to Prince's house. Moisha didn't plan on spending the night but she didn't care because he was leaving tomorrow.

Moments later, they were in his house. Prince immediately got ready for bed and so did Moisha. She got undressed, taking all her makeup off and then put her hair into a ponytail. She put on one of Prince's t-shirt then went back out into his bedroom. Prince was sitting down shirtless on his bed. He was doing something on his phone and didn't even notice Moisha walking in until she got in the bed.

Prince placed the phone down then looked at Moisha. Moisha went over to Prince and gave him a very much wanted kiss. Prince deepened the kiss, adding tongue and putting Moisha in pure bliss. He then got up, grabbed Moisha by her ankles and dragged her to the end of the bed. Going in between Moisha's legs, he got on his knees and buried his face in between Moisha's thighs.

He placed a few kisses on her inner thighs then used his tongue to part her pussy lips. He then licked her pussy from the front to the back, causing her to moan. It was like music to his ears. He began to flick his tongue on her pussy, which made her go crazy.

For the next ten minutes, Prince was doing nothing but devouring Moisha's pussy. Moisha soon came and he slurped it all up. Once he was done, Moisha just laid there. He smirked and then hovered over Moisha, and she was staring at his erected penis.

"Only if you want to," he said.

"Well, I want to," Moisha replied and that was all Prince needed. He quickly got a Trojan and began putting it on. He stroked himself one good time, then proceeded to give Moisha what she wanted.

Prince got in between Moisha's legs once again and rubbed his penis up and down her pussy. He put his penis at her entrance, slowly pushing in.

"Shit," Prince said under his breath Moisha was tight as hell, but he knew she wasn't a virgin.

It only hurt Moisha a little, but once Prince got in tune, it was nothing but pure pleasure. Moisha couldn't deny the fact that Prince's penis was big and she hadn't had sex in three years.

Prince lifted Moisha's legs in the air then picked up the pace. "Uh," Moisha moaned numerous of times.

Prince could feel himself about to release, so he did a few more strokes and after that, he released and then got up to dispose of the condom. Moisha was worn out, truth be told. She got up and went to the bathroom, closing and locking the door.

Prince went ahead and changed the comforter then laid down. After about ten minutes, Moisha still hadn't come out of the bathroom and Prince began getting worried. He soon got up and went to the bathroom.

"Baby," he said, trying to open the door but it was locked.

Moisha opened up the door. "What's wrong? Did I hurt you or something?" he asked concerned.

"No, no," Moisha spoke. "I just feel like if we are going to be sexual then we definitely need to know for sure if this is what we want," she said.

Prince nodded his head. "Well, this is sure as hell what I want."

"I want this too," Moisha said and they shared an embrace.

"Do not be scaring me like that."

Moisha laughed. "I'm just dramatic, that's all."

After their moment, they both went back to bed. It felt good to sleep in Prince's arms; she felt safe and secure.

***

The next morning, Prince woke Moisha up to breakfast in bed. "Good morning sleepy head," he said, placing the pancakes and sausage on the nightstand. After he gave her a kiss on the forehead, he went back to packing. Moisha looked at her phone then began eating. "So, what you have planned today after I leave?" Price asked from his closet.

"Well, I have to get more pant suits for work because I found out that I only have two, so I'll probably go to the mall or outlet," she said.

"Well, if you need anything, just let me know, even if it's money," Prince explained. "I'll give you one of my debit cards," he then said.

"No, it's alright Prince," Moisha said, declining his offer.

"Nah, I insist baby girl. Let me do for you," he said, then came back out his closet to see Moisha was done with her breakfast.

"Alright, if you say so," Moisha said. She was truly grateful for Prince. "What time you leaving today?" she asked, getting up to throw her plate in the trash in the corner of his room.

"One."

Once Prince said that, Moisha looked at her phone to see it was going on ten o'clock.

"Need me to drop you off at the airport?" she asked and he nodded.

"Yeah, let me go ahead and tell my nigga he do not have to," Prince said.

Moisha went into the bathroom and began to wash her face and brush her teeth. She did have a toothbrush over here and a couple of pieces of clothing. After taking care of her hygiene, Moisha put on some sweats and, of course, one of Prince's shirts, then went downstairs to put on her Roshe's. Moisha grabbed Prince's key to his Range Rover then went into the garage to wait on him.

She saw Prince come in the garage dressed in an all-black Nike sweat suit with his all black 5's. He put his suitcase in the back then got in the passenger's seat.

"So, how long is this trip?" Moisha asked, as he let the garage up with the clicker.

"Just two days... Nashville again," Prince said.

"That's not bad," Moisha replied, then plugged up her phone to the AUX.

Prince groaned because he knew she was about to play some 'niggas ain't shit' type music. She went to her K. Michelle album and hit shuffle.

Long distance in the way of what could be
Even when you're here, you're not with me
She's having the child I should've carried
I'll be damned if yall get married
How's the baby, How you adjusting?
Ain't gon work, you got problems trusting
Let me stop, I'm supposed to be focused
But these nights are the coldest

Will you ever let her go? I do not know
Will I ever be first? I hope
But I ain't just sitting around, can't wait for someone to see my worth

Damn I can't compete with a baby

Is there any room left in your heart for me

Prince kept a flat face the entire time. "I love him, I love him, I love him, I love him, love himmmmm. Maybe I should call," Moisha sung K Michelle's *Maybe I Should Call*.

Prince turned off the radio and Moisha griped, "What?" She laughed.

"Let me pick a song," Prince said and grabbed her phone.

"Since you about to leave, I guess." Moisha rolled her eyes playfully. Migos began to blast out of the speakers and Prince began bobbing his head. Moisha was a fan of Migos, so she bobbed her head too.

Soon, they pulled up curbside of the airport. "Thanks baby girl," Prince said, then leaned over and gave Moisha a kiss.

"Bye boo," Moisha said and her face kind of saddened.

"Bye, I'll text you when I land," Prince said, then got her suitcase out the back. Prince began walking towards the entrance and Moisha went ahead and took off going to her home. She wanted to take a shower then go to the mall. On her way back, she called up Zara.

"Yes?"

"Zara, you better not be in yo' lil feelings again. What I say last time?" Moisha explained.

Zara sighed. It was true, it's just EJ. "Girl. I'm sorry... but EJ is going through some shit right now and I'm helping him out," Zara explained.

"Really?!" Moisha said surprised. "Why though?"

"Because I cannot help it! I love him and I want to see him do better," Zara explained, "Mo, you honestly wouldn't understand," Zara said.

"Well, I understand bullshit," Moisha said, sounding purely annoyed. The line went quiet and Moisha knew she struck a nerve. "All I am saying is do not let EJ bullshit you. You saw how much he loved you by when his shit got raided; he won't even trying to save you. He's selfish," Moisha stressed.

"Let me say this again… no one is perfect Mo' damn! EJ and I may not have the perfect relationship but I love him, and he loves me," Zara stressed and then hung up.

Moisha just rolled her eyes. Zara was going to have to see for herself. She just didn't want Zara hurting no more than she already was. Zara was a hothead, so she did what she wanted. Moisha was well aware of that also.

Zara didn't need anyone else questioning her, she got that enough from EJ. Zara really felt as if Moisha didn't understand because Moisha hasn't been involved with man, like Zara has with EJ. So, she had no room to talk, in Zara eyes. If anything, Zara didn't want to stress herself out and end up losing her baby.

Zara did CNA work at a Nursing Home for older people. It was alright for now, but nonetheless, it got the bills paid. Zara had just got done with a patient then her phone began to ring. "Hello?"

"Aye, you need some more snacks," EJ said.

"When I got pregnant, I cut the snacks out. Well some… you hungry?" Zara asked, purely concerned.

"As hell!" EJ snapped back.

Zara exhaled. "There should be some leftovers in the refrigerator, if not, check the cabinet beside the stove," Zara instructed.

"Aight…" EJ replied then hung up.

The call ended and Zara exhaled then rolled her eyes. She was feeling a bit used but she knew that EJ loved her; he just had a very rough time showing it.

Zara was not a jealous type of person, but life for Moisha was much easier than her and that was okay because she knew that trouble do not last. Moisha was a good friend, she couldn't deny that at all, but there were many ways that they couldn't relate.

Moisha grew up in a household with two parents. Zara grew up with her father and didn't really know her mother. Moisha went to college and got a degree. Zara went to college, dropped out her sophomore year, then took classes so she could become a CNA. It was something quick and didn't require ample amount of time. Despise their differences, Zara knew that all Moisha wanted was the best for her.

***

Moisha just got out the shower when she realized her phone was ringing. She put on her soft, plush house coat then answered it; it was her mother.

"Mo?"

"Yes, mother?" Moisha answered, going back to her bathroom to dry off. She put her phone on the counter and then put it on speaker.

"I have the day off and I was wondering if you felt like helping me with the garden in the backyard?" Faith asked.

Moisha looked at the time; it was like one in the afternoon, so she would be able to help her mom out then go to the mall. "Alright, I'll be there in about twenty minutes," Moisha replied then hung up the phone. She quickly got dressed in grey leggings and a black tank top then put back on her Roshe's. She grabbed her black Michael Kors tote then went ahead and exited her home, getting into Prince's car.

She made her way over to her parents' house, thinking about Zara. She truly just wanted the best for her and it seemed as if she wasn't seeing that EJ was using her. It was obvious as hell; she was just blinded by love.

Moisha pulled into her parents' driveway, parked, and got out.

"Whose car is that Mo'?" her mother asked, coming outside.

"My friend's," Moisha replied.

"Mhm, friend. I can tell it's a man friend. Look at those rims," she pointed out, which made Moisha laugh. Moisha locked the car then followed her mother into the house. Moisha closed the door.

"You the only one at home?" Moisha asked her mother, sitting her purse on the couch. She followed her mother out to the backyard and saw the part where she was trying to do her garden. Her mother already had dug out the spots of where the plants would go; she just needed them in their designated spots and then some mulch on top.

Moisha got some gloves and got to work. She put an old towel on the ground, so she wasn't sitting directly on the grass. Her mother joined her and soon, they were planting and carrying out casual conversation.

"So, who is this friend?" Faith asked her daughter. Moisha smirked because she knew this question was coming.

"It's a man, of course, and we have been spending some time together," Moisha admitted.

"Is this the same man which took you on that date?"

"No mama, this is another man," Moisha corrected.

"Hmm… what's his name?" she asked.

Moisha replied, "Prince… he is twenty-seven-"

"Twenty-seven?!" her mother yelled.

Moisha nodded. "Mom, I am twenty three."

"Yeah, I know. That's a bit gap. So, when am I going to meet this man?"

"When we make thing official, we're just taking things slow right now. Still getting a feel for him." Moisha smiled.

Faith was happy for her daughter. She wanted Moisha to find love, in the right places though. "Well, as long as he is treating you right baby, and I can tell you really like him. Have you told your father?'

"No, not yet but I do plan on it," Moisha replied.

Moisha and her mother talked the entire time as they were getting the backyard garden together. She asked Moisha what she was doing for the rest of the day and Moisha let her know she was going to the mall to get some clothing for work, and her mother asked to tag along. Moisha really didn't mind; she hasn't been around lately due to spending so much time with Prince, so she was all for it.

Once they finished up the garden, her mother cleaned up and then was ready to go. They then remembered that Mya would soon be getting out of school and picked her up first.

"Girl, is this Prince's car?!" Mya said, once she got into the car.

Moisha nodded. "So, Mya has met this friend huh?" Faith said, a little jealous.

"Mama, he got money! Let me tell you; his house is huge and he owns Heaven's Kitchen," Mya explained.

"Well damn, Mya," Moisha said, giving her the side eyes as she drove.

"Okay. I've heard enough. I have one question though Moisha?" her mother asked.

"Yes ma'am?" Moisha said, sounding annoyed. She was very annoyed with both her sister and mother.

"Where is this friend at?"

"He is on a business trip," Moisah replied.

"Mhm," her mother replied. Everyone in that damn car was a drama queen; you could tell they were all related.

***

"I do not know how you live with her," Moisha told Mya. They were in Saks watching as their mother tried on different dresses for church.

"Me either, but do not forget you use to too," Mya replied back.

"Ma, I'm about to try some things on also," Moisha said, getting up from the chair. She had three pantsuits she wanted to try on.

Moisha changed out of her clothes and then put on the nude pantsuit, she came out to show Mya. "Do you like?" She asked her.

"Yeah... your booty looks big. I say get it," Mya said.

"I say do not," Faith said, coming out the dressing room. Moisha was surely going to get it. Fifteen minutes later, Moisha was done and ready to pay. Her total came up to twelve hundred and she got out Prince's card and swiped it. She signed his name and the card was approved. The clerk gave Moisha the receipt then gave her the bag, which housed all three of her pantsuits.

Faith then paid for her dress and all three of them left. "Where to now, driver?" Faith asked her daughter.

"I'm going to drop you two off then go back home. I need a nap or something!" Moisha exclaimed.

"Awh. Alright," she replied.

Chapter Seven

A Couple Days Later…

Today was the day. Moisha was going to be starting her first day of work. She had been looking forward to this day for two months and was ready to work. Moisha had set hours, which were from ten to four every day. She was all jittery inside, she had been waiting for this day for forever and it was finally here.

Prince had spent the night last night; he was just getting back from his trip. He groaned. "Why you up so early?" he asked, sitting up in the bed.

"Prince, I do start my job today." Moisha smiled, coming out her bathroom. She only had on her bra and panties, since she was just getting out the shower.

"Oh shit, you excited?" he asked her.

"Of course, now let me finish getting ready," she replied then went back into the bathroom to brush her teeth and take out the flexi rods.

The curls were a little too tight, so Moisha began to brush them out some but nonetheless, they came out flawless and Moisha loved them.

"Mo', see what time your lunchbreak is and I'll bring you some Heaven's," Prince said, as he was on his phone.

"Alright, thanks boo," she replied, then went into her closet to the purple pantsuit she planned on wearing her first day. She had the bottom on when she walked back out to her room to get a white tank top.

"Baby girl, I'm getting ready to head out. Let me know your lunch again," Prince said.

"Do not forget your debit card," Moisha reminded him.

"Didn't I tell you that you can keep it?" Prince asked matter-of-factly.

"No," Moisha replied; she didn't remember Prince saying she could keep it.

"Well, you can keep it. The max on it is about ten thousand. I'll always pay on it," he said.

"No... Prince," Moisha whined.

"Mo'. Please let me do for you... I just want to do for you," he said, going over to her. He wrapped his arms around her from the back, placing kisses on her neck. "I want you to have a good day at work. Aight?" Prince said to Moisha. He went in her bathroom to take a piss and brush his teeth real quick.

"I'll hit you up later baby," Prince said, giving Moisha a quick kiss. He left and Moisha finished getting ready. She went to lock the door behind him then came back to her room to put on her gold flats. She knew now to wear heels on his first day because she didn't know how much walking she was going to be doing. Moisha had a box with things she wanted to decorate her cubicle with, o that was in a little box. After grabbing her purse and the box, Moisha was out the door.

***

The moment Prince got home, he got a call from Xay. He was the watchful eye for Zara, so this must had to be important. "What's up?"

"Boss, can you come down to the trap? I have some information for you," he said and Prince responded, telling him he was on his way. Prince never conveyed information on the phone for security purposes because ain't no telling who else on the phone. The feds really do be listening. Prince went right back out the door he just came in. He got in his car and made his way to the trap to see what information Xay had to tell him; it better be good.

About fifteen minutes later, Prince was there and getting out the car. He went around back to get in. "Xay!" Prince yelled to let him know he was here. Prince looked around and everyone was doing their designated work.

"Right here," Xay said. The two of them went into the back room, so they could have some privacy. In the back room, there was a big round table. Prince sat down and so did Xay.

"So, what's up?" Prince asked him.

"I think EJ is with Zara," Xay said.

"How do you know it's him?" Prince asked. He just wanted to make sure before he made any moves.

"I figured you were going to say that so here," Xay said and then presented Prince with a numerous amount of pictures.

Prince nodded with a smirk. "That's who we need. So, I need to figure out how we're going to do this," Prince said, stroking his goatee.

Zara was Moisha's friend, so he didn't want to do anything to harm her. Prince figured they were going to have to catch that nigga out of Zara's place, which probably wouldn't be hard.

"Easy. Go to that house," Xay said, thinking it was easy.

"Can't. That's my shawty's friend. I do not want to hurt her, fuck up her place, or anything," Prince admitted.

"Wait, wait... you fucking with Moisha?" Xay asked and Prince chuckled, avoiding the question. It was, in all honesty, none of Xay's business.

Prince's phone vibrated with a text from Moisha.

Hey boo my lunch is at 1!

Prince replied back with a kissy face emoji then cut his phone off, placing it back in his pocket. Prince was done talking with Xay, so they both exit the room. Prince went to the packing room, so he could get him a blunt or two. He just wanted to relax and be high real quick. After getting his gas, he went to his car and then made his way to *Heaven's*. He just figured he would hang out there until it was time for him to take Moisha's food. As he drove to the place, he couldn't help but to think about his mother. He missed her truly.

"Prince!" Heaven screamed from the porch. Prince was outside playing basketball in the street.

Prince noticed his mother calling him and quickly left the game. "Yes ma'am?" he asked, clearly out of breath. Prince was like any other twelve year old. He liked playing sports and hanging out with his friends.

"Help me out with this pie, mama trying out a new recipe," she rejoiced.

Prince groaned then turned around, looking at his friend play basketball. "Come on baby, it won't take too long," she said and they both went back into the house. Prince always got teased for cooking so he felt as if he needed to gain his manliness back, which is why he started trapping.

"You know Prince. Women love a man that can cook," Heaven explained to her son.

"But aren't women supposed to do all the cooking mama?" Prince asked his mother,

"Well, not exactly. Now, ain't nothing wrong with a man cooking okay?"

"Yes ma'am," he replied back.

"Now, get me the milk out the refrigerator," she instructed.

When Prince looked back on his childhood, he realized that it was his mother's food that provided for them. She always was selling plates. Even though she worked at a restaurant, his mother had a side hustle that paid just as much as her full-time job.

Prince was finally at *Heaven's*. He swerved into the parking lot, cut off his car, and went in. It was a good handful of people this morning; Price hung his head as he went straight back to the office. He got his key out, unlocking the door then went in to sit down. The moment he sat down, there was a knock. "It's open," he said and in came one of the waitresses, Taylynn.

"Hey Tay." Prince smiled.

"Hey, how are you?" she asked.

Taylynn was about twenty and a single mother of two. Prince often helped her out here and there by giving her money and/or extra hours when she did have a babysitter.

"Good, what about yourself, everything okay?" he asked concerned. Taylynn was like a little sister to him. Little did he know, this 'little sister' had a crush on him.

"It's alright, I can't work that double this Friday though. I do not have a babysitter anymore," Taylynn explained.

"I can find you a babysitter if you really trying to pull this double," Prince said, thinking about Moisha.

"I really am, I need the money." She laughed, but was dead ass serious. "But I do not want just anyone watching my babies," Taylynn added.

"It's not just anyone, it's my girl," Prince said.

His girl, Taylynn repeated to herself in her head. That hurt a little but she didn't dwell on it too much.

"You taken now?" she asked with a smile, which was slightly fake.

"I sure ain't single." He laughed.

"Well, who is she?" Taylynn asked.

"Well, she comes in a lot, you might have seen her. Chocolate tone skin, slim waist, thick thighs. Round face, at the time, she had about shoulder length hair-"

"Oh, the one that never pays for her food when she comes," Taylynn said. Price could detect the sudden attitude.

"Is that a problem or something?" Prince asked, hoping there wasn't. Even if Taylynn did had a problem, it wasn't going to change anything.

"No," Taylynn said.

"I'm not about to make my girl pay for food at a place I own. That's dead," Prince chuckled. "You off?"

Taylynn nodded. "Yeah." Prince nodded.

"If you want, you can go with me to give her some food on her lunch break. You know, just to meet her," Prince said.

"Sure, why not?" Taylynn replied.

Prince got Moisha's food then made his way down to her job. Taylynn looked around Prince's car, it was nice. She could tell he was living in luxury. Prince waited along with Taylnn outside her building in the nearby parking lot.

"She should be coming out, I just sent her a text," Prince reassured.

Taylynn nodded her head, then looked to her left seeing the woman who would get free food.

"Hey baby, I have someone I want you to meet," Prince said to Moisha.

Taylynn looked at Moisha and couldn't help but to notice how beautiful she was. Her skin complexion was literally the color of a Hershey.

"Hey, how are you, I'm Moisha." Moisha smiled.

"I'm Taylynn," she replied.

"Yeah, she works at the dinner and needs someone to babysit," Prince explained. Prince knew that Moisha loved babies.

"Awh, how old are they?" Moisha asked. She definitely didn't mind helping Taylynn out, even if she didn't know her.

"Two and six," Taylynn smiled. She had two girls that looked so much like here.

"Well, I do not mind at all," Moisha admitted.

"See, I told you," Prince teased at Taylynn. "How's work going baby?" Prince asked Moisha.

"It's good; I love it so far. One of these days, you have to come and see my cubicle. I decorated it and it's bomb." Moisha smiled. Prince could tell she was excited. He was happy for her.

"Awh, well I'm happy for you baby girl. Oh yeah, here's your food and let me know when you get off," Prince told Moisha.

"Alright, bye, and it was nice meeting you Taylynn." Moisha smiled then began walking back into work. She had about ten minutes left and she figured she would spend that eating. Moisha went back up to her floor and to her cubicle. The cubicle was a nice size, pretty spacious, and it was a good amount of privacy. Her cubicle, of course, came with a desk, chair, and an Apple desktop computer, but Moisha decorated it in pink, zebra print, and black. It came out nice. She had a pink covering for her keyboard and placed one picture of her family on one side and a picture of Prince on the other side. For the most part, everything was simple. You were given articles to edit then you would submit them to the publishing department. Pretty straight forward. Today, Moisha's supervisor let her take this day to get used to being in her cubicle and getting familiar with the floor.

Four o'clock came along and Moisha was headed out. She grabbed her purse and went towards the stairs. She could have taken the elevator but she was just on the second floor. Moisha was ready to go home to relax the rest of the day.

***

"EJ, what the hell?" Zara yelled, as she came back to her home. Shit was everywhere and gnats were flying around. One thing Zara didn't do was keep a nasty ass apartment, so this was unacceptable.

"What Zara?" EJ stressed, coming down the hallway.

"What you do to my shit?!" she asked, placing her purse down on the kitchen table.

"I had a few of the boys over-"

"Without my permission. Really EJ!" Zara yelled. She exhaled. "Look, I'm going to go to my room to sleep because my feet fucking hurt and when I wake up, my apartment better look clean or else you are going to have to find somewhere else to go," Zara stressed. EJ was about to say something but Zara put her hand up, signaling him to shut the fuck up, and he did as so. Zara walked to her room and shut the door, slamming it and hoping EJ could hear. This was too much and Zara didn't need to stress about anything else. After stripping her scrubs off her body, she got into bed and rubbed her forehead, due to the headache that was present and she couldn't even take any pain killers, this was killing Zara. Slowly but surely, her eyes closed, leading her into a well needed slumber.

***

Moisha sat in bed with the tub of Neapolitan ice cream in between her legs. She turned on Netflix and began relaxing. As she flipped through the Netflix titles, she heard someone come into her house. The only person that had a key was Prince, so she knew it had to be him.

"Baby girl!" he yelled.

"I'm in the room," she replied back. Moisha then saw Prince enter her room, smiling. "What you so happy for?" she asked.

"Why you not?" he asked her. He then cut the light on. "Why is it so dark in here?" He looked around, noticing that she was in bed with ice cream. "Everything alright?" he asked her.

"Yeah, I'm just on my period," Moisha groaned.

"Oh," Prince said. He then sat on the bed. "So, you doing this for the rest of the day?" he asked for clarification.

Moisha nodded. "Don't have shit else to do," Moisha replied back.

Prince exhaled. "Well, thanks for helping Taylynn out. I gave her your number to contact you the day of," Prince explained.

"Alright," Moisha replied.

"Well, I'm going to head on out. You do not seem to be too interested in me being over here," Price said and Moisha exhaled.

"I told you. I'm on period; I just want to relax babe," Moisha clarified.

"Why didn't you just say that?" Prince asked. He removed his shirt, shoes, and pants to get in bed with Moisha.

"Wanna hear the story about how my mama caught me having sex?" Prince asked, trying to lighten up the mood.

Moisha cracked a smile and laughed. "Sure."

Prince began telling the story and for the remainder of the night, they told each other funny childhood stories. Moisha felt as if she was getting to know Prince well. In all honesty, she grew to love him but she felt as if it was too early for all of that. Prince was the type of man she could talk to all day. She really enjoyed his conversation; he was also funny and very outgoing.

"It's not funny," Prince said with a straight look on his face.

"But, but… she made you wear an apron." Moisha laughed. "So, is that why you love cooking so much?" Moisha asked, putting two and two together.

Prince nodded. "Yup. My mother always told me that women love a man that could cook."

"She won't lying either," Moisha laughed.

"See, my mama had me in the kitchen more than anything. I thank her for it though." Prince smiled.

"Your mother seemed like an amazing woman." Moisha smiled.

"She was," Prince replied.

"If I may ask, how did she die?" Moisha asked. She was a little curious since Prince never talked about his mother's death.

"Natural causes or at least that is what the doctors told me," Prince explained and began to tell Moisha the story.

"Yea, let me get about two grams?" one of Prince's regular customer's asked. Prince quickly did the drug transaction then watched as the man walked off. Prince hadn't even been in the game a whole six months and he was already the hottest plug around.

Prince turned around and began walking back to his house, which wasn't far from the block he sells from. He was walking and since it was just beginning to get dark, the street lights began to cut on. Prince knew he had to provide for him and his mother, so this was the only way. It was in his environment and he was a product of his environment.

He pulled out his key and unlocked the door. "Mama!" Prince yelled, shutting the door. It was odd for her not to yell back. He thought that she was in the kitchen. Prince walked down the hall to the kitchen, to see if his mother was there, and she wasn't. The kitchen was her favorite place so something really was up. He saw how the milk and eggs were out, so she did plan on making something.

"Mama!" he said as he went up the steps. He went into his mother's bedroom. She was laid out on the floor and quickly he dropped down, trying to wake her, hoping that she was just unconscious. He noticed that she didn't have a pulse and he quickly called 911. Prince was scared.

"Oh my God," Moisha said. She could see the hurt in his eyes and didn't want to do anything but console him. Moisha held Prince in her arms tight.

"She was my, everything..." Prince said above a whisper.

Seeing Prince like this and hearing that story just made Moisha so much more appreciative of her mother then she already way. "I try not to dwell on it because of my image. You know I do have an image to uphold," Price said.

"But that's your mother and you are human before anything. It's okay to get sad sometimes," Moisha replied.

"Thank you," Prince said, looking at Moisha.

"For?" she replied back in confusion.

"Just being who you are," Prince said.

"Well, you are welcome." Moisha smiled. "I feel so appreciated by you."

"I do appreciate you. I feel like we need to go ahead and make this official," Prince said.

"That is okay with me." Moisha smiled. Prince leaned in, giving her a kiss.

Chapter Eight

Friday came along early around six in the morning and Moisha started off her day by being in the gym. Her road to being smaller was coming to an end. She had been working out a lot and to be honest, it showed. Moisha was very proud of herself.

Once she was at work, Moisha had no idea that Friday was the day when she got off work at one. It was around one-thirty and Moisha was just getting in her car to go home. Just as she was starting her car, her phone began to ring and it was from an unknown number. "Hello?" she answered, pulling out of the parking spot.

"Hey Moisha, this is Taylynn," Taylynn said into the phone.

"Hey boo, how are you?" Moisha asked, making small talk.

"I'm good. Are you off of work yet?" Taylynn asked.

"Actually, I just left," Moisha told her.

"Good. Well the girls are here with me at Heaven's and I guess you can just get them and take them to your place," Taylynn suggested.

"Alright, that's fine. I'll be there in about eight or ten minutes," Moisha replied and the two ended their conversation. Moisha made her way to *Heaven's*, parking and then killing the engine. She looked up at the sky and it looked as if it was about to rain, so she wanted to make things quick; just in case it did rain.

Moisha got out the car and went inside. As usual, it was semi-packed. *Heaven's* was a very popular restaurant in the Memphis area. She had to give it to Prince, he has done a good job all by himself. Moisha saw Taylynn serving tables. After taking orders, she spotted Moisha. "Hey girl, the girls are in the back office. I'll be back there in a sec," Taylynn instructed.

Moisha pointed to the back past the bathroom and Taylynn nodded, so Moisha went ahead. She heard Prince talking and a little girl's voice.

Moisha walked in and everyone's eyes were on her. "Hey babe," Moisha said.

The older girl of the two turned around. "Hey, I'm Kayla." She smiled.

"And I am Moisha." Moisha smiled, due to how friendly the little girl was.

"That's my sister, Jayla," she said.

Just as Moisha was about to respond, Taylynn came into the office. "Thank you so much for doing this. They have already eaten; you have my number. Jayla's bag is right there but if you need anything, just call me," Taylynn explained.

"Alright, and it's no problem." Moisha smiled.

"Bye babies. Mama has to go back to work," Taylynn said, kissing both her daughters. Moisha loved the sight of Taylynn and her daughters; it was too adorable. The thought of Moisha having her own kids ran in her mind, that was until Taylynn closed the office door and snapped her out of it.

"Come on, I'll help you get the girls in the car," Prince said and all four of them left to go to Moisha's car. Moisha picked up Jayla as Kayla lead the way followed by Prince, who held onto Jayla's car seat.

"Ms. Moisha, you're pretty," Kayla said shyly.

"Thank you," both Moisha and Prince said at the same time, which made Moisha giggle a little.

Moisha opened the back seat door for Kayla to get in. After doing so, she went on the other side and put Jayla in her seat, which Prince already placed down.

"Thanks bae," Moisha said, going to the driver's seat.

"You going to be good?" Prince asked Moisha, and she nodded.

"Yeah, they seem like good girls," she explained.

"Alright, I'll come by later," he replied then brought Moisha to him, giving her a kiss.

"See you later," she said and they went their separate ways.

On the way to her home, Moisha tried to make small talk, of course, with Kayla since she seemed so talkative but that was a somewhat good thing. That meant she could easily make friends.

"So, what's your favorite color?" Moisha asked Kayla.

"I like Pink! Yellow and white," Kayla smiled while replying.

"Mine is pink," Moisha said. As she was driving, she looked in the rearview mirror to see Jayla leaned over sleep. The sight was cute. Both Kayla and Jay favored their mother heavily.

Moisha arrived in her complex and parked, killing the engine. She told Kayla she could get herself out and to wait on the sidewalk in front of the car as she got Jayla out. Once she got Jayla out, she got her bag and shut the door, locking the car.

"Alright, come on," she told Kayla.

Moments later, they were in Moisha's house. Jayla was still sleep, so she figured she would lay Jayla down in her bed. She put her baby blanket over her and closed the door a little, then went back out to the living room where Kayla was trying to work the TV.

"What do you want to watch?" Moisha asked her.

"Princess and the frog," was her immediate response and by that, Moisha could tell she really liked that movie. Moisha soon went to Netflix, putting it on for Kayla.

"Would you like some popcorn too, sweetheart?" Moisha asked Kayla and she nodded. Moisha got up, going into the kitchen and then going to the pantry. She browsed the pantry up and down, then grabbed the popcorn packet out of the box. She then proceeded to the microwave and put it in for three and a half minutes.

As she waited, she looked into the refrigerator but was distracted by crying. She knew that it was Jayla and immediately she went to her bedroom to see Jayla sitting up crying.

"Awhhh," Moisha cooed, as she went over to the bed to scoop Jayla up in her arms. Her cries lessened as Moisha got closer to the kitchen. She got the popcorn out and put it in a bowl. After doing that, she got out a Capri Sun for Kayla. Kids love Capri Suns. She got the bowl and Capri Sun and sat it on the coffee table. "Alright, it's all yours boo," Moisha said to Kayla.

"Thank you." Kayla smiled and it honestly surprised Moisha how mannerable Kayla was.

"You are very welcome," Moisha replied, then began to look in Jayla's baby bag. She saw pull-ups, in hopes that Jayla was potty trained.

"Kayla, is your sister potty trained?" Moisha asked and Kayla nodded. There were two bottles of milk and Moisha got one out and gave it to Jayla. She accepted and everyone was happy.

"Ew, they kissing like mommy and Mr. Prince." Kayla giggled.

"Who is Mr. Prince?" Moisha asked, just a little curious about what she said.

"You know." Kayla smiled.

"So, your mommy and him use to kiss?" Moisha asked, just making sure. Kayla nodded and Moisha made a mental note of that. She would deal with that later.

Twenty minutes later, all three of them were sleep and Prince was coming in and saw the sight. He awwed then tried to sneak up on Moisha.

"What the hell you doing?!" she spat, looking up at him.

"Calm ya tits." He laughed then got some popcorn from the bowl.

Moisha groaned then got up from the couch. "Do you know what time their mom is coming?" Moisha asked Prince, hoping he knew.

"I'm not sure. I know that she gets off at nine," Prince explained, going into the kitchen. Moisha following him going to get a water. He tried to touch Moisha and she shrugged the jester off. He was take back by her action. "What's wrong?" he asked.

"Nothing Prince," Moisha replied in a monotone voice. Moisha's phone vibrated and it was a text from Taylynn saying that their dad was going to pick them up and she needed the address. Misha quickly replied back with her address then placed her phone back down and went into her room. Prince followed her.

"Moisha, if you want me to go, then I will," he explained.

"I mean, if that's how you feel, who am I to stop you?" Moisha asked, looking at him with her hands on her hips.

"You are someone to stop me. Moisha Danielle Thomas, do not even act like this bruh," Prince spat.

Moisha's eyes widened as she heard Prince say her full name. She parted her mouth to say something but her doorbell rung and Prince went to go get it.

He opened it. "What's good bruh?" he spoke to Kayla's and Jayla's dad.

"Hey man. What's good?" he asked him and the girls' dad saw Moisha. "Hey, thank you for watching them," he said.

"It's no problem, they are good babies." Moisha smiled, "And let Taylynn know if she needs a babysitter any other time, I do not mind helping her out," Moisha replied and he smiled. He got the girls situated and soon they left, and it was just Prince and Moisha.

"So, guess what Kayla said while we was watching the movie," Moisha said.

"What?" Prince asked with a blank ass face.

"She basically said you and Taylynn kissed. See, I'm not too much worried about the shit that happened before me but I'm going to just leave it at this. If you feel like some shit like that will happen while you and I are together, then we might as well end this now," Moisha preached.

Prince nodded. "I feel you. I mean, it was only one time. To be quite honest, it didn't even mean shit but when I say you have nothing to worry about, you do not," Prince explained.

Moisha nodded. "Good."

"Is that why you was acting all uptight Mo'?" he asked, laughing. "You've got to be kidding me," Prince said, once he realized that was the reason, since she stayed quiet.

"I mean... I just wanted to know," Moisha said, defending herself.

"Have you spoken to your friend?" Prince asked as Moisha was about to throw the rest of the popcorn away.

"Who? Zara?" Moisha asked and Prince nodded his head. "Nah. She be in her own world some days and I do not visit," Moisha said.

Prince laughed. "Y'all seem so...soo..."

"Different?" Moisha finished for him.

He nodded. "Yeah."

"I mean, we balance each other out. She's my other half," Moisha replied and Prince gave Moisha the 'bitch please' face.

"I'm your other half," he replied with a slight eye roll, only joking. In all seriousness, he wouldn't mind being Moisha's other half one day.

Moisha laughed. "Shut up."

For the rest of the night, Moisha enjoyed Prince's company. Times they spent together were always fun because the both of their personalities mixed so well together. Moisha did really wonder why Zara acted the way she did, especially when it was about EJ. She definitely didn't play about her 'man'.

***

It was Saturday morning and Zara was, of course, off for the weekend, so she did want to go out in just a little. Her first bet was calling Moisha but she figured it was too early and Moisha was always an early riser, so she decided to go to her dad's house.

Zara and her dad's relationship was existent but they weren't that close. Zara's father lived in an apartment about twenty minutes away from her. Once she got there, she knocked on the door. Soon, her dad opened and she smiled. "Hey daddy. How you doing?"

She went inside the apartment, which smelled like pig feet and beer. It was a very unpleasant smell. "How are you doing… the both of you?" He smirked.

Zara smiled. "We're good."

"Is EJ around?" he asked her, opening up his newspaper.

Zara exhaled while sitting down. "He's around," she said. He technically was.

"But is he around for the baby Zara?" he then asked. Zara got silent and her dad put the newspaper down. "Why must you continue to fuck with his no good ass?" he asked, looking directly at Zara.

"Look. I love him."

"And you need to stop," her father snapped.

Zara rolled her eyes. She could feel the tears building up, so she just decided to go. "I'll just leave," she spoke, getting up.

"To go be with that fuck nigga? Come back when you got some damn sense. I raised you with-"

Before her dad could even finish fussing, she left, slamming the door on purpose. Zara made it to her car and broke down. She had the pain EJ caused her built up and she couldn't hold it in anymore. Times like this is when she needed someone to comfort her and she knew it wasn't going to be EJ. She wanted to call Moisha.

Zara wiped her face as she went to Moisha's contact and called her. She put it on speaker and waited for Moisha to answer.

"Hello?" Moisha answered.

"Hey…hey, what you doing?" Zara asked, making small talk first.

"Just got dressed... is everything okay? You do not sound too good?" Moisha asked. She could tell something was obviously wrong with Zara, probably why she called.

"For the most part. Have you ate yet?"

"No, I'm hungry though," Moisha chuckled.

"Meet me at Chick-Fil-A," Zara instructed and Moisha accepted. They then ended the call and she went in the direction of Chick-Fil-A.

Once Zara got there, she ordered her food, got it, then went outside to join Moisha. "Hey boo," Moisha said, looking up from her phone. The two shared an embrace then sat down in their designated seats.

"So, is everything okay?" Moisha asked Zara, she looked a little stressed.

"I visited my dad today," Zara spoke up.

Moisha new from past encounters that, that couldn't have gone well. Zara's dad was too judgmental and opinionated. He was blunt as hell and didn't care whose feelings his words hurt.

"Ooo, how that go?" Moisha asked.

"Bad… said EJ was a no good nigga and he needed to be in the child's life," Zara explained.

"But, that's true," Moisha said, a little confused. "It seems like you running away from the truth with him and you do not want to face the truth with him," Moisha said.

Zara nodded. "But what if people were telling you bullshit about Prince? How would you react?" Zara challenged.

"Well, for one, if people were coming to be about Prince, I would of course ask him and if I witness it for myself, then I would take actions into my own hands. A nigga will do what you will allow them," Moisha explained.

Zara nodded. "You right. I mean, I know how EJ is but I still love him and I want to help him be a better person, not even for me, but for himself," Zara replied.

"But see, you cannot help a person that doesn't want to be helped," Moisha said and Zara got quiet. "I do not want to tell you what to do because I aint ya mama but I will tell you what I think is best for you," Moisha spoke truthfully.

Zara gave a weak smile. "Well, I thank you for that and I'm sorry for closing you out sometime. I know it gets aggravating sometimes," Zara explained.

"It's alright boo. I understand." Moisha smiled back.

***

As Moisha and Zara were having a great time talking amongst each other and catching up, EJ was about to get that ass caught. Xay watch closely as EJ walked out of Zara's apartment, lighting the cigarette. Xay smirked then grabbed the walkie-talkie. "And he is out front," he spoke and then watched as two masked men came out the cut. One punched Xay unconscious then the other did also, just in case the first wasn't enough. Both men quickly dragged EJ's unconscious body to the van and they sped off back to the trap.

Xay quickly called up Prince to tell him the news. Prince was excited he was alive because he had a few questions for him before he got rid of him. Prince entered the trap twenty minutes after Xay called him. There was nothing but evilness in Prince's eyes; once he had his heart and mind set on doing something, best believe he was going to do it.

"Where is that bitch ass nigga?!" Prince asked the moment he crossed the threshold.

"Basement boss," someone spoke, and Prince smirked as he headed down there. He rubbed his hands seeing Xay. Xay dapped Prince up.

"He all yours I gave him a dose of anesthetic, not too much though, just enough for him to be out until you got here," Xay said.

"Thanks, can you hand me my gun?" Prince instructed and Xay followed. EJ was sitting in a chair with his hands handcuffed in the back and his feet handcuffed together by his ankles.

Prince got the water hose, turned it on, and pointed it towards EJ. "Wake up pussy!" Prince barked and EJ's eyes slowly opened. From instinct, he began trying to break free but there was no point. Those handcuffs were top of the line, so he might as well stop.

"Prince, what do you want from me man?" EJ asked out of breath.

"You stole from me and didn't think I would find that as huh?" Prince asked him with a chuckle.

"Look, I'll give you all the money back," he said and Prince began shaking his head.

"No, no, you said that the first and second time. I gave you chance after chance bruh and you fucked me over. I do not like to be fucked over. So, what you think I should do Xay?" Prince asked Xay, who was just coming back with the gun.

"Do what you gotta do boss." Xay smirked.

"Please, I have a child on the way," EJ quickly said, hoping that would mean something to Prince.

"Like you give a fuck," Prince chuckled, "Now, after this, I hope you learned your lesson," Prince said, bringing out the gun and shooting EJ dead in the forehead.

"What you want to do with the body?" Xay asked after the damage was done.

"Burn that bitch. I'm about to go get cleaned up, some of that niggas blood on me," Prince groaned.

Prince loved when he eliminated some of his problems. He felt as if he didn't need anyone or anything stopping him; he terminated shit like that immediately.

Chapter Nine

Moisha got up Sunday morning and decided that she and Prince could work out together. Prince thought it was a great idea because he was already planning on working out today. Moisha got ready, putting on her Nike spandex leggings, sports bra and a hoodie, along with her New Balances.

She got her keys then went to her car to head over to Prince's house, but first she picked up some Starbucks. Then, she proceeded over his house.

"Bae!" Moisha screamed once she was inside. She closed the door and looked all around.

Prince snuck up on her then wrapped his arms around her. He placed a kiss on her neck. "Mmm. You smell good," he complimented.

"Thanks, you do alsos" She said, turning around. She stared at Prince, looking at his body. He was shirtless, only wearing basketball shorts with workout shoes.

"Just to let you know, I am about to work your ass out," Prince chuckled, as he led the way to the home gym.

Moisha shrugged, she needed the work out. "And I'm ready," she challenged.

"You be doing weights also?" he asked, as they entered the room.

Moisha shook her head. "No."

"Well, we can start off by doing that," Prince said, then instructed her to lie down on the bench. "I'm going to start you off at eighty pounds," he said. He then put the rod in her hands. He put each weight on the end.

"Wooh," she expressed, once he took the rod off the stand.

"You got it though boo," Prince said, giving Moisha kiss.

Forty minutes later, Moisha was completely worn out but for some odd reason, Prince wasn't. He was now jogging on the treadmill. "You tired already?" he asked while laughing.

Moisha gave him the side eye then rolled her eyes. "I need to shower. I'm done," she said then went upstairs to Prince's room. She went into his bathroom and closed the door. She stripped out her clothes then got into the shower.

After she lathered her body up with Victoria's Secret Sweet Pea body wash, the shower door opened and she knew it could be nobody but Prince, naked as the day he was born.

"So, I guess you done too?" Moisha asked and he nodded, standing right behind her as he let his hard penis poke her ass.

Moisha giggled because she knew what Prince was trying to do. "Let's wait until we get out... you know what happened last time," Moisha groaned and Prince began to laugh. The last time they tried to fuck in the shower, Moisha slipped and didn't even want to fuck anymore.

"It's not funny," Moisha said and Prince began washing her back and she did the same to him.

"Alright baby girl... I'm done with it, for now," he said, smirking.

***

Zara got up in the morning and there was still no sign of EJ. She began to get worried. Usually, he would be back from wherever he was at by now. She began to call his phone and she heard something vibrate in the bathroom. Zara scrunched up her face and began walking to the hallway bathroom.

There it was. EJ's phone. She grabbed it and immediately started going through it. Besides all the conversations with females, there was one message that did catch her eyes.

Bruh, I heard Prince is out to get you, you may need to leave that bitch house and go somewhere else.

"Bitch?!" Zara said to herself. She then braced herself because she began to read the rest of the conversation, everything from this week. It began to hurt Zara because EJ really didn't give a fuck about her. She then began to call the guy; she had to know what happened to him.

"Aye EJ, bruh, I thought they gotchu' fam!" he said into the phone.

"And I think they did," Zara said, shocking the hell out of him.

"Wait, wait, who is this?" he asked Zara.

"Zara," she replied.

"Zara who? Oh wait, EJ's shawty," he said, shrugging it off.

"Don't say that when in y'all text messages you was referring to me as a bitch!" she snapped. "But anyways... EJ has not came back and I am worried, and I was wondering do you have an idea or happen to know where he could be?" Zara asked, hoping he knew something.

"To be honest as hell ma', Prince probably got him."

"And did what to him?" Zara asked, not knowing what answer to expect.

"Killed him."

Once Zara heard that, everything went into a blur. She couldn't imagine the thought of EJ being dead, it was heart stabbing. From that point on, everything seemed to be moving in slow motion and Zara figured she just needed to lay down somewhere. EJ's death was so heavy on her mind that possible reasons began to cross her mind and she wondered why Prince would do such a thing.

Zara began to develop a hate for Prince. She didn't care if that was Moisha's boo thang or not. He killed the only man she really loved and her child's father. This was all too much to take in at the moment. The only person that knew about Zara and EJ was, of course, Moisha. Zara began to think. Soon, overthinking landed the idea in her head that Moisha told Prince about EJ being with Zara.

"Would Moisha really do that?" Zara thought to herself. Or she just could be completely tripping. She hoped that Moisha wouldn't rat EJ out like that though. Zara exhaled then picked up her own phone calling Moisha. She didn't get an answer, which irritated her.

Next week was Moisha's birthday, so she figured she would give her a break and then ask her about it the after.

***

Monday morning, Moisha was in a great mood. It was her birthday week and sex with her man started it all off right. She was in her cubicle ten o'clock in the morning, finishing up some edits from the week before.

"Here Mo', these are for you." The mail person came by placing the white Roses on her desk.

She smiled. "Thank you." Even though the flowers were absolutely gorgeous, she couldn't keep them because that would be disrespectful to Prince. She already knew they were from Wesley, like last time before. She then looked at the notecard and saw a crown on it.

What the fuck Wesley? Moisha thought to herself then just placed the flowers back down, out of the way of her working. Moisha went ahead and picked up her phone to call Prince and tell him.

"Hey baby," Prince said, answering the phone.

"So, I just wanted to go ahead and tell you that someone, well I know who it is but anyways, this man named Wesley just sent me flowers, and I wanted to let you know," Moisha replied.

"White Roses?" Prince asked.

"Yea. How you know?" Moisha asked, a little concerned.

"Baby, I sent those. Shit. I sent some to your house before," Prince admitted.

"It was signed anonymously?" Moisha asked, hoping Wesley didn't lie about flowers.

"Yup… all me," Prince replied.

"Wow… another dude said he sent me them. He just straight lied like that, wow," Moisha admitted.

Prince smacked his teeth. "Yeaaaa, but baby go ahead and get back to work. I'll talk to you later," Prince said and hung up the phone.

The nerve of Wesley, Moisha thought. If he lied about something as simple as flowers, then what the hell else he lie about?

Prince got off the phone with Moisha to do more planning for her birthday. He wanted it to be big; he was trying to bring the whole city out. It was official. He and Brando had a night club, which was called LIT. Prince and Brandon made sure that every night the club was open, it would be LIT. They already had a line of promoters working for the club. Prince went ahead and made Moisha's birthday bash the grand opening night, so this was about to be epic. Prince had been planning this since Moisha told him her birthday.

Prince was on the way to the club to meet the planner to just have a walkthrough. The club was nice and there was a big ass parking lot beside the building, so there would be no need for parking on the street. Of course, there would be valet parking.

Once Prince parked his car, he killed the engine and got out. He already saw the event planner out her car; she was in the front with her notepad ready to go. Price got out the keys to the building and went up to the front.

"How you doing, Angela," he spoke to her as they shared a quick side hug.

"Great. Prince, this looks nice," she said while looking at the all-black building with black pillars. Prince went ahead and unlocked the door, opening it for Angela. They both entered. When you first stepped in, there was a foyer with bathrooms and the offices. Going into another door, they went into the big open space.

"Wowwww," Angela commented. She looked around seeing the bar, stage, and obvious VIP areas. "The go-go dancers can go on those poles in the middle. Everything works out perfectly," Angela said. Prince just stayed in the back and let Angela do her thing. He went to his office, looked around, then got the flyer the CEO of the promoting team gave him, so Angela could look at it.

He left the office with the flyer then went back out to the club area. "Prince, I wanted to kind of decorate the VIP area where Moisha was going to be," Angela called out to him.

"Go for it. I trust your skills," he replied. Everything was falling into place and it was a good feeling.

Chapter Ten

"Moisha, what you want for your birthday?" Mya asked, as she and Moisha were watching 'Jane the Virgin' on Netflix.

"I do not know. I'll be fine with whatever you give me," Moisha spoke, not taking her eyes off the TV.

"Well, nothing it is," Mya smiled while teasing her. Moisha then turned away from the TV, giving Mya the side eye. Moisha's birthday was this Friday and she was turning twenty-four. She was exited, even though she probably wasn't going to do nothing; it was good to live another year.

"What's your plan for your birthday?" Mya asked.

Moisha paused the TV. "Nothing at the moment," she replied truthfully.

Truth be told, Moisha wasn't very big on celebrating her birthday. Over the years, her birthdays didn't really go as planned, due to circumstances and financial issues. She was happy to even get a dinner.

Growing up, money wasn't really plentiful. Luckily, her father moved up in the corporate world and her mother was able to keep her little accountant job, but for a middle classed family, they all turned out just fine. When Moisha was younger, she often complained about not being able to get the things that she wanted but as she got older, she understood that she had everything that she needed.

"You already know Prince is taking you out," Mya said with a smile.

Moisha smiled also. "Yea but even if he were to not take me out, I wouldn't be upset or anything," Moisha replied.

"Mo', I think y'all may get married," Mya prophesied.

Moisha exhaled. "Day by day. We're taking it day by day," Moisha told her.

Mya nodded. "Okay and I feel like y'all are going to get married. Which needs to hurry, I want a niece or nephew," Mya said and Moisha began laughing.

"And you'll get one in like ten years," Moisha reassured, then got up to go into her bedroom. She looked at her phone, realizing that after about five messages, Zara had not replied to them. She called Zara two times and didn't get an answer. She would do a popup at her house today but she figured she would do that tomorrow after work.

"Mya, you do not have school this week, right?!" Moisha yelled out.

"Hellllll to tha' naw!" Mya yelled back. Moisha already knew that meant Mya was spending the night. Mya got up and went to Moisha's room. "We should cook tonight and invite our men." Mya smiled.

Moisha looked at Mya as if she way crazy. "You have a man?!"

"I mean, he's just a friend but I like him." Mya blushed.

"Aweeee, let's do it. Throw on your shoes and let's head to Walmart!" Moisha said as she got up.

***

"So, what do you want to make?" Moisha asked Mya as they walked down the bread aisle. Moisha put some hotdog buns in the basket.

"I think we should do lasagna, I mean everyone loves lasagna," Mya spoke.

"Alright, alright. Let's do it," Moisha spoke then they went to get some ground beef. Moisha was looking for ground beef in the raw meat section when she heard someone speak her name. She turned around with a confused face, looking all around.

Moisha noticed Wesley and her eyes widened. "Hey," he spoke with a smile.

"Hi," Moisha said quickly.

"Long time no see or hear from," he chuckled.

"Hey, I'm dating dating someone, so... yeah," Moisha replied nervously.

"Oh." Wesley's face fell. "Well, it was nice seeing you," he replied with a faint smile, walking off.

"Won't that nail shop man?" Mya asked with a confused look upon her face. Moisha just nodded and then Mya dropped the three pounds of ground beef in the cart.

"My My, you can pick up some snacks too," Moisha told Mya.

She nodded. "Well, you go get everything for the lasagna and I'll get snacks," Mya said, going another way. Moisha made this little grocery trip quick because she didn't want to be cooking all night.

Moisha paid for the groceries and then, she, along with Mya, made their way home. The moment she and Mya got back home, they washed their hands and began cooking. Moisha began making the sauce and Mya began to cook the meat. The prep only took about fifteen minutes, afterwards, there were ready to layer the lasagna in a pan.

Once they were done with that, Mya went into the refrigerator, getting the salad mix and began to prepare that. Moisha left the kitchen and began to call up Prince.

"Hey baby!" Prince answered and Moisha smiled.

"Hey, you want to come over for dinner?" she asked him, already knowing he will probably say yes.

"Eh. Baby, I'm sorry, but I have some business to handle tonight. Save me some," he said and Moisha's face instantly fell, developing a frown.

"Ok. Bye," she said then hung up. Moisha left her phone on the charger then went back into the kitchen where Mya was on the phone. You could easily tell she was talking to her little crush because she was smiling and blushing.

Mya ended the call. "Text me your address." Mya cheesed.

"So, is Prince coming?" Mya then asked and Moisha shook her head. Mya didn't say a word after that because Moisha didn't look like she was in the best mood. On the bright side, Moisha got a chance to see the boy her little sister was dealing with.

Moments later, there was a knock on the door, "It's Jaylen!" Mya rejoiced. Moisha thought it was cute. Moisha watched as Mya opened the door and there revealed a tall, light skin boy. He looked like a little player.

"Mo', this is Jaylen. Jay, this is Moisha," Mya introduced the two.

"Hey." Moisha smiled.

"Hey… you two look so much alike," he complimented.

"Okay... that's enough." Mya rolled her eyes, making Moisha laugh.

"I cooked everything and I hope you like it Jay." Mya smile and Moisha looked at her as if she was crazy, but she stayed quiet.

"Aight ma', just do not try to poison me," Jaylen joked.

"If that's the case, then the both of us will be getting poisoned." Moisha laughed along with Jaylen.

"Okay... y'all," Mya said and everyone began to eat.

"So, how old are you?" Moisha asked Jalyen. Mya gave her the side eyes. "What?! I'm just making some conversation," Moisha protested.

Jaylen chuckled. "I'm seventeen," he replied.

"Oh junior," Moisha replied and Jaylen nodded.

"He is going to be a pro basketball player." Mya smiled.

"That's what you want to be?" Moisha asked and he nodded. "So, do you have a backup plan?" she asked.

"I'm pretty sure I'll make the NBA," Jaylen replied and Moisha was impressed. He was determined as hell.

As they all ate, they still had small talk. Moisha soon learned that Jaylan was the captain of his school's basketball team and he already had scouts looking at him for college, which was good but it was always good to have a backup plan.

"Well, you seem like a nice boy... well, for now. I have work in the morning so goodnight you two," Moisha said as she got up.

"We'll get the dishes, if there are any," Jaylen spoke up.

"Ooooo, I like you," Moisha said over her shoulder as she went down the hall to her room. She went into her room then closed the door, hoping to have some type of notification from Prince. She checked her phone and there was nothing, so she figured she would call. They always talked on the phone before they went to sleep.

The phone began ringing as Moisha sat on her bed; she exhaled as it went to voicemail. She figured she would just go to sleep and try again before she went to work.

Morning came around and the first thing Moisha did was take a shower. After she took a shower, she stood in front of her mirror, looking at the hickeys that trailed up from her belly bottom to the middle of her breasts. Prince was something ese. Moisha put on panties and a bra, brushed her teeth, and cleaned her face. After doing her hygiene, she went to her phone to see if she had some type of notification from Price and she didn't, so she went ahead and began calling him.

"Hello?" he answered in a sleepy voice.

"You must forgot about me?" Moisha asked, as she went into her closet.

"Nah, I was actually going to call you when I woke up but I guess this is cool too," Prince chuckled and Moisha rolled her eyes.

"I have some leftover lasagna for you. If you want it," Moisha said. From her closet, she picked out a pink skirt with a black and white striped shirt along with black wedges to match. Moisha wanted to switch it up for her birthday week.

"Yeah. I'll come by after you get off," he replied.

"I'm surprised," Moisha mumbled, not expecting him to hear.

"What was that?" he asked and Moisha quickly replied nothing. She didn't feel like arguing with Prince today, maybe tomorrow.

Once she was ready, Moisha then went in the guest room to see that Mya was knocked out. She laughed lightly to herself then grabbed her purse and keys, leaving the house.

The day went by slow as ever; Moisha felt like she had been editing for hours and hours. She was honestly feeling really tired. Even though she was sitting down, her feet began to ache. When her lunch time rolled around, she didn't even eat; she was just ready to go. Moisha did make it in her plans to go visit Zara to see what was up. Lately, she really hasn't been the same and it was worrying Moisha.

It was like she would go ghost, apologize for going ghost, then go ghost again, and then apologize for doing so. It was really starting to worry Moisha. Then again, Zara is pregnant, so it may just be hormones. Moisha at least wanted to give her the benefit of the doubt.

The moment the clock hit three-fifty Moisha was already logging off of her computer, but was disturbed by a tap on her shoulder.

"Ms. Thomas, could I have a moment with you in my office. I know you are about to go; this won't quite take long," Moisha's supervisor spoke. Moisha nervously got up and followed her; she didn't know what was about to happen. If she were to get fired, her parent's would be so disappointed in her. She hasn't even been working here for a month.

Her supervisor opened the door, holding it so she could come in. "Take a seat," she then suggested and Moisha did so. "You are not in trouble," was the first thing she said then laughed.

Moisha blew out a breath of relief then smiled. "Yes, Mrs. Hills."

"Well, I was looking through your edits and I just wanted to commend you myself. You are doing really well for someone who is coming straight out of college. Keep up the work and in another three months, you'll probably get a promotion." She smiled and so did Moisha.

"Thank you, Mrs. Hills, it means so much. Best believe I will continue putting forth one hundred and ten percent into my edits."

"Good to hear. Have a good day Ms. Thomas," She said and Moisha knew that was her cue to go. She waved goodbye then went back to her cubicle, officially leaving.

Opening her door to her car, she felt good about work and felt like she could see herself staying at this job for a long time. Once in her car, she made her way to Zara's apartment, hoping for some answers. Soon, she was there and Zara's car was there, so she just knew she would answer. Moisha went up to her door and began knocking on it.

After five minutes, Moisha began to say, "Zara, I know you hear me out here! You know what. You bipolar as hell!!"

Moisha yelled then made her way back to her car; she wasn't about to waster her time anymore with Zara.

"Bipolar bitch!" Moisha spat as she got into her car. She quickly called Prince. She just needed to vent and when he didn't answer, it pissed her off even more. Prince was acting a little different too. Shit, in Moisha's eyes, everyone was acting funny, but that was alright because she was about to go ghost.

She began making her way home in a rage. The moment she stepped foot in her house was the moment she realized that she just needed to go to sleep and try again tomorrow. "Mo', you alright?" Mya asked, going into her sister's room.

"Yea," she said.

"Welp. I'm going home now," Mya said, turning around. Moisha stayed quiet.

Mya's car was finally out the shop, so she was able to drive around, not relying on her parents and sister anymore. As she got into her Honda Accord, she noticed that her gas light was on. She exhaled then made her way to the closest gas station. About six minutes of driving was behind her, she found a BP and pulled up beside a pump. The closing of a door snapped her out of her thoughts; she recognized it was Zara and smiled. "Hey Z baby!!!" she yelled.

Zara turned around with a look of fire. "Tell Moisha the next time she want to bang on my door, she'll get something that she ain't knocking for," Zara griped.

Mya scrunched up her face. "Which will be?" she asked curiously. Mya rode for her sister, so she was doing exactly that with Zara.

"Stay out of grown folks' business." Zara laughed.

"Stay out of abortion clinics," Mya spat back with a low blow but she ain't care. Zara was Moisha's friend, not hers.

Zara waved her off with an attitude then went on ahead out of the store. Mya rolled her eyes then tended to pump the gas and, of course, she was going to tell Moisha about her this little encounter.

The week flew by quickly and soon as Moisha knew it, it was her birthday. Just her luck, her supervisor let her have the day off. Moisha was really grateful and she was still able to get paid. Throughout this week, the only people Moisha was really communicating with was her mother and, of course, Mya. Prince was so damn busy this week, it was ridiculous. Even when she went by *Heaven's*, he wouldn't even be there. Mya told Moisha what happened between she and Zara. Instantly, it made Moisha pissed.

It was around seven in the morning and Moisha's phone began to ring. She didn't have to be up for work until like another hour, so whoever this was, it better be good.

"Hey," she answered in a sleepy voice.

"Moisha! I forgot to tell you but last night, I saw Zara," Mya said.

Moisha sat up. "And what happened?"

"Well, I didn't know y'all was beefing so I spoke... you know how I am. She was like... 'Tell Moisha the next time she want to bang on my door that she'll get something that she ain't knocking for' and you know me Mo'. I was like which is because I'll be damned if I won't stick up for you," Mya explained.

"Wow... and I do not even know what she is mad for Mya. I really do not," Moisha replied.

"Let 'er stay mad. With 'er made ass!" Mya said.

Just the thought of it made Moisha's skin boil. Something was obviously wrong with Zara. She just ain't up and get mad, saying shit like that for no reason. See, if

Moisha was a hothead like Mya, she probably would have just went back to Zara's apartment like '*What's really good bitch?*' but that wasn't the grown woman way to handle it. So, Moisha would just give Zara her space.

Moisha put all the bullshit behind her and continued getting her feet done, along with Mya. Mya was treating, which surprised Moisha.

"Mommy and daddy wanted us to go by their house because they have something for you," Mya sang.

"What they get me?" Moisha asked. She knew Mya would tell because she could hardly hold water.

"I do not know. Dead ass. I think they didn't tell me on purpose because they know I would probably tell you," Mya said, then sucked her teeth afterwards.

"This is all your fault," Moisha teased. Mya exhaled with a laugh.

Thirty minutes later, Moisha and Mya was out of the Nail Span and on to their parents' house. Moisha noticed her brother's car and looked at Mya as she looked to her.

"Mat!" they both said at the same time, then exited the car.

Moisha locked her car door then followed Mya into the house. They both went into the living room and saw their parents speaking with Mat, and his facial expression wasn't a good one. He looked horrible and as if he hadn't slept in days.

"The birthday girl is here!!" Marc rejoiced.

Moisha gave a light smile. "Thank you, daddy."

"Happy birthday lil sis," Mathew then said afterwards.

"Thank bro, you alright?" Moisha asked. Birthday or not, she was highly concerned.

Mathew exhaled. "Well Moisha, Ashlynn took the girls." Faith said Mathew instantly and Mathew yelled out in frustration.

"What?! But why though? She just upped and left?" Moisha asked. She knew that those girls are Mat's world.

"Look Mo Mo... I do not even know. A divorce may be near because I'll be damned if she takes my babies away from me. I tried calling and she ain't even answering. Like what type of shit is that?!" he explained.

"Baby, just cool it. I mean, they have to come home tonight," Faith suggested to her son. "Well Mo', we have some gifts that you might like baby," Faith said, getting up. Moisha smirked then followed her mother. She followed her up the steps and into the master bedroom. One the bed laid two presents and Moisha knew they were both for her.

"These two are from me and your father," Faith explained with a smile. "Open mines first." She smirked.

Moisha looked at her mother weirdly, accepting the box. She ripped open the gift and it was a Victoria's Secret lingerie piece. Moisha gasped, "Ma!"

"I know, I know, you love it," Faith said. Moisha picked up the black lace bra and lace panty thong. It was cute; she couldn't even lie.

"Thanks ma." Moisha smiled, then opened her father's gift, which was a Michael Kors handbag that she adored. You could tell it was pretty pricey.

Moisha took her gifts as she went back down the steps. "Thanks daddy!" Moisha said, then kissed his cheek.

"And she ain't answer again," Mathew said, slamming his phone down on the coffee table.

"So, ya' mother told you what to do, just keep calm," Marc stressed.

"Aight, aight." Mathew surrendered.

Mya went ahead and went upstairs to her room. After twenty minutes, Moisha went ahead and went back to her home to relax. Prince had been MIA the whole day and hadn't told Moisha happy birthday. Once she got home, she noticed the white rose petals that covered the floor.

She was a little confused so she, of course, followed the rose petals to her room. Her door was slightly cracked, so she went ahead and opened it. Just as she suspected, it was Prince. He was lying down on her bed sleep.

"Prince, get up!" Moisha yelled, going over to him and shaking him.

Quickly, Prince got up and looked at Moisha with a smile. "Hey baby. Happy Birthday!" he said, getting up and going over to her.

"Prince, can you just leave me alone. I want to be alone; this has been a long week" Moisha explained to him then went into her room.

"Is that so?" Prince questioned, following her. He then wrapped his arms around her. "So, you want me to leave you alone?" he asked, pressing his hard dick on her butt.

Moisha turned around, giving him the side eye because she knew exactly what he was trying to do.

***

"So, is that a yes?" Prince asked Moisha after they were done with three rounds. It was exactly an hour later.

"Yes Prince." Moisha lughed.

Prince kept on asking her to go out with him to his club's grand opening. Moisha soon gave in, saying 'yes' especially after the hot, steamy sex they just had. She could have said yes to anything.

"Good," he said and kissed her. "I have some gifts for you too baby. You know I didn't forget at all," Prince said and Moisha watched as he got up going to the gifts he hid in her closet.

Moisha looked in the bag to see an all-white, strapless Gigi dress. In another bag, there were Jana Leather strappy sandals. Moisha looked at him. "Babe, you shouldn't have," she said.

"But I did and you're going to wear this tonight," he said.

Moisha exhaled. "Alright. We got to shower," Moisha said and the two of them did just that. Once they showered, Moisha began to wash her face and apply her makeup, which took no longer than twenty minutes. Once her makeup was done, she just flat ironed her weave then began putting on her clothes.

Prince, on the other hand, been ready. He was sitting in the kitchen taking shots of Hennessy, waiting on Moisha. He was dressed in a white Gucci, button up shirt, light washed True Religion jeans, and tan Magnanni loafers. He intensified his look by adding a gold chain and gold Versace watch.

Moisha was finally done and decided on gracing Prince with her presence. "Wow," was the only thing that left his lips as he stared at his girlfriend.

"Baby, you look so beautiful. Twenty-four looks good on you," he complimented.

"You smell good," Moisha complimented. She could tell it was his usual Ralph Lauren men cologne.

"You ready?" he asked and Moisha nodded.

It didn't take them long to get to the club. Prince pulled up in front of the club in his Porsche. Moisha felt honored to even ride in it; it was nice. He pulled up to the walet, which was complementary for him. You could hear music from the outside as well as see the long ass line that nearly wrapped around the building.

"Good ass turnout," Prince said, mentally patting himself on the back.

Prince dapped up the security and bouncer at the door, then went right on in. "Baby, this is nice," Moisha spoke, as they went into the club area.

Prince held onto her hand as they maneuvered throughout the crowd. Moisha noticed as he got so many 'heys' and 'what's ups; she knew just from that that Prince was a very well-known man. Soon, they went to a secluded section, which was the obvious VIP area. The security guard saw Prince and instantly let him in.

Moisha looked around, taking the scenery in. There were pink balloons and even a pink 'Happy Birthday' banner. Moisha knew this only wasn't his club's Grand Opening.

"Happy Birthday," various men and women said to Moisha that was in the section.

Moisha didn't really recognize anyone. She did recognize Brandon, which was the only one. She, of course, replied a sweet, 'Thank you' and kept it moving. Of course, there were a few groupies but they were Brandon's groupies.

"Yo, Prince and Brandon, this hot y'all. Congratulations," a man came up to both Prince and Brandon saying.

"Thanks X," Prince replied.

"Thanks man," Brandon said.

"Oh baby, this is one of my good friends, X," Prince introduced the two.

"Hey," Moisha said with her hand out.

"What's up lil mama, happy birthday!" he said and Moisha smiled.

"Thanks."

"X is the owner of a few car lots and if you need something, he could definitely hook you up," Prince explained.

"Hmph." Moisha smiled. She did want another car, something a little more luxurious, but as of now, she loved not having a car note.

There was a bottle of Crown Apple Royal that Brandon gave Moisha for her birthday; he even challenged her saying that he wanted the whole bottle gone. Prince began joking and saying that she couldn't and to prove Prince wrong, she accepted Brandon's challenge. Moisha was definitely not a punk.

"Baby, we'll be back..." Prince said, referring to him and Brandon. They both got up and by passed Moisha. She opened the bottle, taking a swig from it.

"Wooh," she said then twisted up her lips. She sat it down, trying to look for Prince.

The two of them got on stage and the DJ lowered the music. "Aye, aye!" Brandon said.

"What's good y'all?!" Prince said and the crowd clapped, giving the two of them their undivided attention.

"So, y'all liking Club Lit right now?" he asked and the crowd went wild.

"Aint it lit, though?" Brandon asked, and he and Prince shared a quick laugh.

"But, I'm going to need y'all to do a favor and wish my baby-" Prince started but was cut off by Brandon.

"Yeah... his baby, his girlfriend, which means you hoes better stay in y'all place."

Moisha's eyes widened, "Nigga, shut up," Prince chuckled.

"But, I just want y'all to help celebrate her birthday. She's twenty-four today and looks twelve. Shine the light on my baby!" he said and everyone laughed, looking over at the VIP section to see Moisha downing the bottle. Once she noticed the light on her, she smiled.

"Well then," Brandon said.

"Thank y'all for coming. DJ bring that shit back!" Prince yelled and the DJ played Drake and Future's *Big Rings*.

"What a time to be alive!!!" Prince screamed as he and Brandon got back to the VIP section. The moment he went, he downed a shot of Cîroc, then another. He made sure not to get too fucked up. He had to drive.

***

Moisha and Prince left around one and Prince wasn't fully sober but he was good enough to drive. Moisha, on the other hand, was fucked up completely.

"Babyyyyyyy, I love you so much. I liked you coming into my life," Moisha said. She had been saying weird shit the whole way back to her home and Prince had just been ignoring it, but he couldn't ignore what she just said.

"I love you too," Prince replied, meaning every bit of the three words. He couldn't help but to laugh at her choice of words though.

"Baby, baby, baby, baby, babyyyyyyy," she sang along with Ashanti. "I only had one bottle, why da' hell do I feel like a noodle?" Moisha asked with a laugh.

"Um, boo boo, you had two. You had Amsterdam also," Prince said, regretting giving it to her.

Once they got to Moisha's house, Moisha went right to her room and laid down. Prince chuckled because she didn't waste no time. He went into her room and began stripping down to his boxers.

An hour later, he was sleep but Moisha wasn't. She was up and changing out of her dress. Moisha put on some sweats and a regular ass big t-shirt.

Moisha grabbed the keys to her car and left out the house. The slamming of the door woke Prince up and he look to his left and got worried because he didn't see Moisha. "Moisha!!!" he yelled.

He got up and went down the hallway to see all the lights off; he went out the door and saw Moisha leaving fully dressed.

"Bae, where you going?!" he yelled.

Moisha didn't even turn around to acknowledge Prince. She made it to her car and started the engine, in route for Zara's house. Moisha was tired of the shit with Zara and wanted to dead it; yes, at three in the morning.

As she drove, Prince was just getting into his car. He couldn't just leave Moisha out there un-sober. He didn't want her to get into an accident and to make matters worse, he had no idea where she was going.

Moisha pulled up to Zara's apartment complex and got out the car. Just as she was getting out, Prince turned into the complex. Moisha went up to Zara's apartment door and began banging. "Open up bitch! You said you had something for me, then let's go. I do not give a fuck if you pregnant or not!"

"Moisha!" Prince yelled as he got out the car.

His eyes widened. "No, no. You not about to try to fight your friend at three o'clock in the morning," he said.

"Fuck that…. I know you up bitch. I know!!! Probably in their sucking a random ass nigga's dick!" Moisha yelled.

She began to kick the door and that's when Prince needed to get her. He picked her up bridal style and took her back to the car. "Prince, let me go!!" she cried.

"No… Moisha, you need to go to sleep and try this again at another time."

"What the fuck I say?!" she screamed.

"Chill the fuck out!" he barked and Moisha instantly got quiet and cried to herself.

Moisha couldn't hide the hurt she had from not talking to Zara and she didn't even know why. Moisha knew she was a good friend and for Zara not to even talk to her was bogus as hell, and Moisha was hurt.

Chapter Eleven

Moisha woke up the next morning with a very bad headache; she then turned over to see Prince sleep. She snuggled up next to him and laid her head on his chest. He bent his head down, giving her forehead a kiss. The two of them laid in bed for the next twenty minutes. Then, Moisha got up because she had to take care of the headache. First, she went into her bathroom to brush her teeth, then she went under her sink to look for some pain killers. She finally got some. Opening the bottle, she popped two then exited. She went into the room to see Prince on his phone.

"You good baby?" he asked and Moisha nodded.

She then put some shorts on. "Yeah, I have this headache but I just popped some pills, so hopefully they come through in the next two seconds." She laughed.

"So, why Zara text me with some bullshit?!" Moisha then said and Prince laughed.

"Is that who apartment door you were banging on?" Prince asked with a chuckle.

Moisha's eyes widened. "Huh?"

"Last night, you were off a molly." Prince laughed and Moisha then asked what happened. Prince gladly explained how crazy she was acting last night. Moisha couldn't believe it. He was kind of embarrassed.

Moisha laughed then shrugged. "I mean we have to talk to each other sooner or later," she said, after Prince explained.

"But, I told you I loved you?" she asked.

He nodded. "I said it back, though because I do love you."

"To be honest, I been wanted to tell you I loved you but I didn't want to rush anything," Moisha said. Prince understood but he was glad Moisha said it.

Moisha went into the kitchen and decided on making a small breakfast for her and Prince. It was simple; sausage, eggs, and grit. Once she was done, she decided on replying back to Zara's message.

I mean if you want to meet up, it's honestly whatever. Say no more.

Moisha rolled her eyes, pressing send. "Breakfast ready!" Moisha called, so Prince could come. Moisha already had Prince's plate made, alongside with orange juice.

"There you go baby," Moisha said, pointing to the plate. Prince kissed her then sat down and began eating.

Meet me at the city park in like twenty minutes then.

Zara replied and that was good with Moisha, so she replied 'k' and kept it moving. She ain't have time for foolishness.

Moisha went to her room to get ready and once she came back, Prince looked at her like she was crazy. "Where you about to go?" he asked, looking at her up and down.

"Meet up with Zara," Moisha spoke and with the mention of Zara's name, Prince's face flattened. "We're going to talk babe," Moisha reassured him.

"Mhm, if you need me to go, then I will," Prince told her.

Moisha began shaking her head. "No baby, it's good. I'll be back," Moisha said, leaving her condo. She made her way to her car, then to the park. She didn't know what Zara was about to say.

The drive was about ten minutes, so Moisha was there in no time. Since it was a nice day, of course, people were out enjoying themselves. Moisha swerved into the parking space, parking then killing the engine. She exited her car, making sure she put on her sunglasses.

Moisha looked around and saw Zara sitting at one of the benches across from the playground. Moisha made her way over there. "Hey," she said, sitting down next to Zara.

"This really ain't a happy go lucky get together. I just want to ask you one question and if you lie to me Moisha, I'm going to be highly pissed off," Zara explained.

Moisha just waved her off. "Anyways. What is the question?" she asked.

"Did you tell Prince that EJ was staying with me?" Zara asked.

"No… I didn't even know he was living with you. So, do not ask me. What Prince got to do with EJ anyways?" Moisha asked.

"He killed him!" Zara spat. "And you probably helped him!!!" Zara added.

Moisha was taken back by Zara's assumptions. "What type of shit? Really Zara… I'm gone. I refuse to be accused of some shit I didn't do!" Moisha said getting up.

"Bye… watch ya' back bitch and Prince's back too. If you can!" Zara yelled.

Moisha stopped dead in her tracks. She then turned around. "Leave my man out of this."

***

Once Moisha got home, she quickly told Prince everything. Prince was precautious as hell, so he wasn't really comfortable with Zara knowing where Moisha lived. Ain't no telling what she about to do.

"Baby, do not worry, I got it. Do not even worry about it," Prince reassured.

"But did you really kill EJ though, is it truth?" Moisha asked out of curiosity.

Prince exhaled. He really hated mixing business and personal shit together but he just couldn't lie to Moisha. He looked up to Moisha, who had wandering eyes and he then exhaled. "Yea, I did."

"But why? Are you a murderer or some shit, Prince? What do you do for a living? The house, the car, shit, your whole damn lifestyle. I know how we met was a part of your work but damnit, Prince, I know you do not get paid for breaking into people's houses and I know by you owning a restaurant ain't making the money you spending. Prince, what the hell do you do?" Moisha demanded answers and Prince felt as if this day was going to come, just not this soon. He didn't have a problem telling her what he did; it was just a matter of her keeping the shit to herself.

"Aight. Aight!" he slightly yelled, "I run drug operations. Killings, sometime that alone makes money. Dirty money, so I opened up Heaven's and that club to clean some of it up," Prince explained.

Moisha wore a puzzled look on her face. "Confusing, I know. You said you wanted to know so there you go and know I'm going to go, so I can figure out how to handle this situation," Prince said and he left. Moisha was still startled. She basically just lost the one friend she had over a man, but that was okay because Zara didn't seem like a real friend anyways.

Moisha didn't even stop Prince; she just let him leave. Prince got in her car pissed. He knew from this point on shit was about to get crazy and he honestly wanted to leave Moisha out of it. As he drove, he began to go into deep thought about the time he spent with Moisha. She was perfect and he knew he needed her in his life, but he didn't know if she needed him in hers.

Prince tried to keep personal and business separate but he failed, and he felt very bad. He just didn't want no harm to come to Moisha because of him.

He changed directions, going to the trap house. He needed to notify his men about the chaos that was soon to come and for them to somehow put a stop to it before things got ugly. The moment he got there, he called for a mandatory meeting. He told them everything for them to keep a lookout in the streets and to not speak of the name 'Prince' or 'Moisha' to anyone. He also told them to tell him if anything was a little fishy or out of the norm.

***

Moisha, on the other hand, was exhausted. She laid in her bed with an upset stomach. She didn't even have any ginger ale, which was the bad part. It was around eight in the morning Sunday. Her phone began to ring and she exhaled as she picked it up. "Hello?" she answered.

"Moisha... you coming to church?" her mother asked and she shot up real quickly.

"Yea mama, just let me get ready. I'll be over in an hour," Moisha said and began getting out of bed. She hadn't talked to Prince today but she gave him the benefit of the doubt, since it was early in the morning. After she showered and took care the rest of her hygiene, she was ready to put on her Sunday's best. Moisha wore a simple nude dress, red sweater, and red Michael Kors flats. Moisha didn't go to church as often as she should but God was definitely in her heart and a major part of her life. Moisha sprayed on some perfume, putting the finishing touches on her outfit. Once she was satisfied, she grabbed her purse and was out the door. Usually, when she went to church with her family, she would just ride with them.

Moisha got into her car in route for her parents' house; as usual, it didn't take her long to get there. She parked curb side then got out. Just as she was getting out, everyone was coming out, so the must have been waiting on her.

She locked her car then looked to the three of them. "Morning family." She smiled.

Everyone got into her dad's Tahoe and took off to the ten o'clock service. As they road throughout the streets of Memphis, Faith turned aroundand looked at her daughter, Moisha.

"Mo?" she said.

"Yes ma'am," Moisha replied back.

"You're glowing," she complimented and Moisha accepted the compliment with a smile.

"That's good to know because I feel the exact opposite," Moisha sad, referring to her stomach hurting and the drowsiness she felt.

"Is everything alright?" her father spoke up, concerned.

Moisha nodded. "Yeah daddy. I'm alright." They pulled into the church's parking lot and parked. Moments later, they were inside the sanctuary. After an hour of praise and worship, offering, and announcement, the Pastor finally began preaching. Moisha was very attentive but there were a few words that she felt like he was speaking directly to you.

"People come into your life for a season!" Pastor Andy expressed, hearing a few 'amens' here and there. "During that season, they could either teach you a lesson or are a blessing to your life. Saints, I do not want you to mix up the lesson people with the blessing people!"

Some people began standing up and clapping. "But wait, there's more. Just simply ask God to point him out! Tell God to show you who is meant to be there and who is not!"

Moisha listened attentively to Pastor Andy's message, it truly spoke to her. Church this lovely Sunday was truly needed. In another thirty minutes, church was over and the Thomas family was in route to get something to eat.

Mya got to choose the restaurant and she chose TGI Friday's, which was alright because everyone was able to get something off that menu. Soon, they were seated with their drink orders already in place.

"Can I talk to everyone about something?" Moisha asked and they all nodded.

"So, I am thinking about moving…" Moisha trailed off.

"What?!" Faith exclaimed.

"To where, baby girl?" her father asked.

Mya just rolled her eyes. "Well, not too far. Jackson Mississippi maybe," Moisha explained.

"But why?" Faith asked.

Moisha began shaking her head. "I just need to get away from things. I love you all, I truly do, but I want to start living for Moisha. Honestly, I want to do what I want to do," Moisha said, hoping they would understand.

"Really Mo'? You want to leave me?" Mya asked, looking at her sister.

Moisha looked at Mya and saw nothing but herself. She damn sure ain't want to break out in tears right here in the restaurant but she felt them coming.

"Mya, I have too. I need to get away," Moisha explained.

"What about me?" Mya expressed and everyone at the table could tell she was on the verge of tears.

"Mya, you know I love you so, so much. You can visit me anytime. Shit… if you want, you could live with me." Moisha smirked and so did Mya.

"Oh hell no," Marc said.

"Y'all chill out. It's Sunday," Faith said, referring to her husband and daughter's choice of words.

"Another thing, I do not know if I'm sure yet. It's just a thought and I wanted to let all of you know," Moisha said.

Soon, their food came and the family began eating with a wave of silence over the table. Everyone had their own feelings towards Moisha's previous statement.

***

The whole day Sunday, Prince stayed cooped up in his bedroom smoking. He didn't have time for anyone or anything. It was just him and hit thoughts. He wanted to stay with Moisha but he felt as if he was no good for her. She even said it herself; it was because of him that she lost a friend. For some reason, when she said that, it hit him hard, real hard. Prince tried to shake the shit off but he couldn't.

He couldn't even deny the fact that spending time with Moisha had been some good ass times and Price hadn't really enjoyed himself since his mother's death. With Moisha, every day he learned something new and his love for her got stronger.

Prince inhaled the marijuana, letting it set, then exhaled. He began to think the unthinkable; he just may have to let her go for the sake of her. The life Prince lived was not a life Moisha needed to be a part of. Without further thought, Prince called Moisha. This would be his first time contacting her today.

"Hello?" she answered.

"Hey, hey. Can we talk sometime today?" he asked, getting straight to the point.

"Sure, sure," Moisha said. She told him that she was on her way home and that she'd be at his house in about twenty minutes.

Prince began to air out the house as much as possible before she came over because he was pretty sure it reeked of marijuana in his home.

Moisha pulled into Prince's driveway, unsure of what he had to talk to her about, even though she felt as if she had an idea. She went into the house with an open mind.

Moisha knocked on the door, not using the key he gave her because she felt as if she may be giving it back. Soon, Prince came to the door and Moisha noticed how much he didn't look like himself. His skin looked a little pale, his eyes had eye bags under them, and she could tell that he needed to go to a barber.

"Why you ain't use your key?" he asked, as she went in.

Moisha closed the door. "Because I didn't want to."

She followed Prince to the living room, where the two of them sat down. There was silence as Price rubbed his hand over his face. He couldn't muster up the words to tell Moisha how he felt, for some reason.

"So, what's up?" Moisha asked and Prince exhaled.

"I think you should get all your things from over here," he mumbled but Moisha heard him loud and clear.

"I do not think I'm for you," he then spoke and Moisha's mouth parted but no words came out of them except a noise.

"Hmm?" she was confused.

"Your life seemed to be good until I got in it and I'm going to solve the problem by subtracting myself," he explained.

"Your house key," he said, placing the key to Moisha's condo on the coffee table.

Prince didn't say another word but Moisha was broken. She couldn't even describe the state of mind she was in right now; her body went numb as to her feelings. Not saying another word, she placed Prince's key down, picking up hers. She headed up the steps to get the clothes and shoes she had over here.

Once she was done, she made it to her car, putting the things in her backseat. The second she got into the driver's seat, she slammed the door and cried her heart out. Moisha placed her forehead on the steering wheel, letting the tears flow. Five minutes into crying, she brought her head up and took a tissue out the glove compartment and wiped her face with it. She couldn't sit in his driveway forever, so she began backing up to go home. The whole way home, she couldn't find an ounce of joy to be happy about. To top it all off, she didn't even have no one to talk to, so she had to bottle up her emotions.

Once she was home, she got comfortable and then grabbed her laptop and began looking for a home in the Jackson, Mississippi area. Maybe, she really did need to move.

Chapter Twelve

Moisha went to work the next morning like any morning, but unlike the others, she was hiding her emotions behind a fake smile. Today, she wanted to ask her supervisor, well talk to her about how she planned on moving. Her supervisor let her know that since there wasn't an office to where she was thinking about moving to that she would have to work from home. Moisha didn't mind at all. She just may have to make this move. After work, Moisha even planned on changing her number. As she was working, her phone began to ring.

"Moisha Thomas," she answered.

"Mo'!" Mya said.

Moisha lightly smiled. "Hey boo!"

"So, since you plan on leaving me, can we spend a lot of time together?" she asked Moisha and Moisha laughed.

"Of course. You think I was really going to leave with spending time with you, little girl?" Moisha laughed.

"I mean... ain't no telling." Mya laughed.

"Whatever, let me get back to work. After I get off, I'll come get you," Moisha said.

"Alright, I love you."

"I love you too," Moisha replied. Moisha placed the phone back on the hook then got back to work, thinking about how her life is about to change drastically, but that was alright.

Moisha got off at three and just like she said, she picked Mya up from their parents' house. "So, where is

Prince? Usually you two will be all up under each other like it's not hot outside," Mya said.

"We broke up," Moisha said. She couldn't believe she just said those words; it just didn't seem real to her.

"What... the... fuck? Are you serious?" Mya asked surprised.

"Yup, yup," Moisha sighed.

"... is that why you are moving?" Mya asked.

"Um, a little bit," Moisha replied, telling the truth.

Mya just stayed quiet as they pulled up to the AT&T store. Mya was confused as to why they were here but she stayed quiet. Moisha parked the car then looked to Mya saying, "I'll be right back," and then went inside.

No longer than fifteen minutes, Moisha was out with her new number. "So, why you had to go in there?" Mya asked; she was curious.

"Just got my number change. The only people that will have it so far is, of course, you, mommy, and daddy," Moisha explained to Mya.

Mya felt as if there was something big happening that Moisha wasn't telling here. Moisha was doing too much shit but Mya put the thought to the back of her mind and just looked out the window watching the scenery of Memphis as Moisha was driving.

Once Moisha was home, she wanted to show Mya the loft floorplan she planned on getting.

"Wow, so you are going to have a room for me? You shouldn't have," Mya teased, as she noticed there were two rooms on the floor plan.

Moisha gave her the side eye. "It's a guest room," Moisha said.

"Mhm, do not lie to ya' self, Mo', but I'm about to go cupcake with Jay on the phone," Mya said and skipped down the hallway to the guest room. Moisha smiled, looking at how happy her sister was. She began to figure out what they were going to eat. Moisha wanted some soul food so that meant *Heaven's*.

"I'm going to Heaven's!" Moisha yelled, letting Mya know.

She knew that she may have a possibility of running into Prince if she goes to *Heaven's* but she didn't care because she could simply ignore him. Moisha got into her car, letting the windows down so she could feel the nice warm breeze. It was September and the weather in Memphis was good. Not too hot or cold, just right.

Soon, she was swerving into the parking lot. Once she was parked, she got out, closed the door and locked it. She entered the restaurant and many of the employees began speaking to her.

"Hey Mo, the usual?" Taylynn asked and Moisha nodded with a smile. "And also add on Mya's usual too," Moisha said.

"Prince is in the back, so go ahead and wait for your food back there girl." Taylynn winked and Moisha chuckled.

"I'll stay up here."

Taylynn's eyes widened. "Alright mama." Taylynn put in Moisha's order then began making small talk with Moisha. During their conversation, Moisha didn't bring up the status of her and Prince. It really wasn't everyone's business.

"The girls miss you," Taylynn said as she got Moisha a drink.

"Awe, I miss them too. I'll come by and see them before I move," Moisha said.

"Move?" Taylynn repeated. "Where you moving too?" she asked.

"Jackson," Moisha replied.

"Mississippi?" Taylynn asked for clarification and Moisha nodded. Taylynn then got Moisha's food. "Alright girl, here you go," Taylynn said, handing her the bag.

"How much?" Moisha asked as she grabbed the bag.

"Girl, do not play dumb. You know you do not pay." Taylynn laughed.

"Tay, let me pay." Moisha and Taylynn went to the register to ring Moisha up.

"And that'll be thirteen dollars and forty-three cents," Taylynn spoke. Moisha handed her a twenty dollar bill and then told her to keep the change.

Taylynn watched as Moisha left and once she did, she went into the office to speak with Prince. "So, you and Moisha not together anymore?" she asked him.

"Nope," he said, popping the 'p'.

Taylynn sucked her teeth. "And you fine with that? You basically led her on-"

"Look, mind your business Tay!" Prince barked. Taylynn rolled her eyes.

"Better get her because she's a good woman. I could tell she loved you and plus, she's moving, so if you plan on getting her back, you need to do it fast. You do not miss out on having someone like that in your life," Taylynn preached then left the office.

Taylynn's words did linger in Prince's head but he decided to show his feeling at a later time. Until then, he began preparing all the employee's checks for payday on Wednesday. As he did so, he began to think about Taylynn's words. Prince didn't want to lose Moisha at all; he just felt like he was doing her a favor by leaving her alone because that's what she made it seem like needed to happen.

Prince, of course, missed Moisha, her touch, her smell, shit; everything about her. He picked up the phone, calling her so he could satisfy the need to hear her voice.

"Hello, the number you are currently trying to reach is out of service. If you feel as if you have got this message as an error, hang up and try again," the message said. Hearing that broke Prince's heart because that meant she changed her number.

Prince exhaled dramatically then finished up his work. It seemed as if Moisha was gone for good out his life.

***

Moisha got home to see her sister, Mya, and her "friend" Jaylen on the couch watching a movie. "Here's your food Mya and hey Jaylen," Moisha spoke.

"Hey Moisha, how are you?" Jaylen asked.

"Good. Well, I'm off to my room," Moisha said then went to her and slammed the door with her food in hand. She stripped out of her clothing and began to lay in bed. Moisha quickly turned the TV on as she placed her food in front of her.

And I'm so sick of love songs, so tired of tears
So done with wishing you were still here
Said I'm so sick of love songs, so sad and slow
So why can't I turn off the radio?

The radio wasn't even on but Ne-Yo's *So Sick* was in Moisha' head. She decided to turn the TV off and go ahead and play the song on her phone.

Gotta change my answering machine, now that I'm
alone
'Cause right now it says that "We can't come to the
phone"
And I know it makes no sense, 'cause you walked
out   the   door
But it's the only way I hear your voice anymore

It's been months and for some reason I just (Can't
get   over   us)
And I'm stronger than this

No more walking round with my head down
I'm so over being blue, crying over you

And I'm so sick of love songs, so tired of tears
So done with wishing you were still here
Said I'm so sick of love songs, so sad and slow
So why can't I turn off the radio?

Gotta fix that calendar I have that's marked July
15th
Because since there's no more you, there's no more
anniversary

I'm so fed up with my thoughts of you and your memory
And now every song reminds me of what used to be

That's   the   reason   I'm
So sick of love songs, so tired of tears
So done with wishing you were still here
Said I'm so sick of love songs, so sad and slow
So why can't I turn off the radio?

Leave me alone

(Stupid love songs)

Do not make me think about her smile

Or having my first child

Let it go

Turning off the radio

'Cause I'm so sick of love songs, so tired of tears
So done with wishing she was still here
Said I'm so sick of love songs, so sad and slow
So why can't I turn off the radio?

Said I'm so sick of love songs, so tired of tears
So done with wishing she was still here
Said I'm so sick of love songs, so sad and slow
Why   can't   I   turn   off   the   radio?
(Why can't I turn off the radio?)

And I'm so sick of love songs, so tired of tears
So done with wishing you were still here
Said I'm so sick of love songs, so sad and slow
Why can't I turn off the radio?

(Why can't I turn off the radio?)

Why can't I turn off the radio?

By the end of the song, Moisha was in a fetal position crying. She missed Prince so much but she wouldn't dare call him or go see him. Moisha felt the hurt all over again, as if she was sitting in his living and was telling her how he felt. Moisha was so heartbroken and truth be told, Prince was too.

Chapter Thirteen

1 week later…

"Baby, that is all!" Marc said as he brought the last box into the living room.

"Thanks daddy," Moisha cheered as she looked around. The loft wasn't bad at all; it just needed a touch of Moisha on it. The loft was really open. It was two levels and all the appliances were up to date. Moisha had been in Jackson for all of two days and didn't think it was that bad. Of course, it was nothing like home, but it could take some getting used to.

Moisha planned on painting the walls in the living room and kitchen red, her bedroom was going to be painted nude and the guest room was going to be painted chocolate. The painters were coming Tuesday of next week and Moisha was excited; she felt as if she was making her own moves making her feel very independent.

"Mo', this is nice!" Mya complimented.

Throughout the process of Moisha moving, her family was a huge help and she couldn't thank them enough. Throughout the whole weekend, they helped her move her furniture from her condo into her loft. They even helped place the furniture in its rightful place.

Moisha went up to the master bedroom with Mya hot on her heels. "This is so big," Mya said and she walked through it. There was no balcony like in her condo but there was a widow seat. The balcony was in the living room, which was fine.

Hours and hours of unpacking and moving Moisha's home looked somewhat presentable and she knew once it began to get dark that her family had to leave.

Saying goodbye to basically the only people that she knows was going to be beyond hard. Moisha's mother, father, and sister piled into the now empty U-Haul and Moisha, being the cry baby that she is, began to cry.

"Baby girl, we are only three hours away," her father said with a chuckled.

Moisha cracked a smiled then nodded. "Alright. I love you guys and drive safe," Moisha said and they took off back to Memphis.

It was now just Moisha and her loft. She went back into her building and up to her new home. The moment she entered, she began going to the bathroom. She had to throw up; she couldn't hold it in anymore.

Once she was done throwing up, she washed out her mouth then began brushing her teeth. She went to lay down on her bed. Her mind went to how she and Prince met; that day was so crazy but so life changing.

"Look around the house, I do not think anyone is here," a smooth, husky voice said. Moisha's plans to get up from the table was changed. Before, she was going to stay her ass down there.

"Nigga, I think the cops coming," another voice spoke.

"Yeah, yeah, keep watch out. I'll look my damn self," the voice replied. Moisha could hear his steps wandering, then wandered themselves over to where she was. She tensed up then paused her breathing, so he wouldn't hear. Moisha slightly turned to the left and could see the black Gucci Loafers.

"Whoever this is...he got money," Moisha said in her head, she dared not say it out loud though.

"Really," he said and squatted down to Moisha's level.

Moisha began to slightly laugh. Soon, she began to look at how her body had changed and realized how she was late for her period. At this moment, Moisha was thinking the worst.

***

Back in Memphis, Prince was sitting outside of Moisha's old condo, which was unoccupied, little did he know. The whole week, Moisha had been the only thing on his mind. He finally put his pride aside and decided to go pay her a visit before she moved.

Even know it took him a week, he didn't think she would move out that quickly. Finally, he got out his car then onto the front door. He knocked and waited, knocked twice then waited. Someone was coming out of the condo next to hers and began laughing. "You looking for the chocolate thang with the fat ass?" the man asked.

Prince looked at the man like a fool then nodded. "Yeah."

"She moved out... maybe like two... three days ago," he chuckled and kept on walking. Prince was crushed; he had no idea how to get in touch with Moisha's family or how to get in touch with her. Once Prince got back into his car, he really hated to do it but it was time to move on. It was obvious that Moisha did and he should do the same. Once Prince got home, he went up to his room and turned on the news.

"Breaking News! Near downtown on West streets. Whitley Condominiums No deaths or injuries have been recorded, stay tuned."

Prince side eyed the news then turned the TV off. He knew for a fact Zara probably had something to do with that. Then he began to be glad that Moisha wasn't living there anymore because she could have been hurt or worst case scenario, be dead.

He then cut off the TV and made a few calls. He felt as if he needed to keep another eye on Ms. Zara. She was very sneaky and it was obvious that she was working alongside someone. Prince was going to find out and put a stop to it all. Even though he and Moisha may not be cool at the moment, he still was going to make sure no harm came her way.

Prince planned on getting Moisha back, slowly but surely. He had to find out where she was first, if anything.

Chapter Fourteen

Moisha looked at the home pregnancy test and exhaled. How could she be so carless? Moisha was, in fact, pregnant but she just wasn't sure about keeping the baby.

Working from home was so much more convenient, Moisha loved it. She was able to just get up and walk a couple of steps straight to her computer. Moisha began editing two articles. Alongside with editing, she was thinking about what to do with her current situation. She and Prince were probably never going to speak again, so why keep this baby? It was such a bad time to have a child and Moisha knew that she wasn't ready to raise a baby but before she made any decisions, she wanted to fully think it through.

It was around lunchtime and Moisha was getting hungry; she saved her edits then put on her shoes and grabbed her purse. She decided on going to Walmart to get something to eat.

Once in the car, Moisha put in the nearest Walmart in the GPS. It was only eight minutes away, which wasn't bad. She began making her way to Walmart, swerved into the parking lot, parked, then got out, locking the doors.

She grabbed a cart and proceeded to the frozen foods sections. Moisha grabbed some simple Eggo's and then went to the noodle aisle. She decided on making spaghetti; it was quick, delicious, and simple.

Moisha was done with her grocery shopping and decided to go ahead and get in line. Luckily for her, the lines weren't that long and it was only one person in front of her. Soon, they were out the way and the worker was scanning her items. Moisha paid forty dollars then was on her way back to her car. She opened the back seat, putting each and every one of her groceries in the back. She closed the door and heard a voice say, "I got the cart." Moisha quickly turned around, so she could put a face to the voice. There stood a man around her chocolate complexion that was about six feet even.

"Oh, thank you." She smiled.

"It's no problem." He smiled, turned around, and took the cart elsewhere. Moisha got into her car in route for her home. Upon making it home, Moisha turned on her speakers, plugging her phone into the AUX, so she could play some music as she cooked. Tory Lanez's *Say It* blared out the speaker system as Moisha put the noodles onto the boiling water. Just as she was cooking the ground beef, her phone began to ring with a Facetime from Mya. Moisha put the meat on low then went over to her phone and answered the Facetime.

"Mo' Mo'!" Mya yelled.

"Hey boo!" Moisha said while laughing, looking at her sister.

"I smell what you burning all the way in Memphis. You need to stop," Mya teased.

"Girl," Moisha replied, giving her a 'bitch please' look.

"But Mya, let me tell you something. Don't tell mommy or daddy. Okay?" Moisha said in all seriousness as she looked Mya in her eyes at the screen. Mya nodded.

"I'm pregnant," Moisha said lowly. Mya's mouth formed the shape of an 'o' and Moisha began to nod. "But here's the bad part, I don't know if I want to keep it," Moisha said and Mya's mouth formed into an even bigger 'o'.

"All jokes aside Mo', do what you want to do. It's your body and you know whether or not you are able to take care of a child at this time. So shit, I say do what your heart tells you to do," Mya said and Moisha cracked a small smile.

"That's sister. Your input means a lot to me," Moisha said.

"Well baby, have a nice night and text me in the morning," Moisha said to Mya. They then shared their 'I love you's' and were off the phone. Moisha was done with her meal and began eating. As she ate, she tried to do some editing and she also wanted to do some research on abortion because she thinks she wants to abort the baby.

She figured that the timing wasn't good and that Prince didn't really want to deal with her at the moment and to bring a baby into all this shit would be horrible.

Moisha definitely wanted to have a baby, but right now wasn't a good time at all.

***

A couple of days later, during the midday, Moisha had made an appointment to have her abortion. She was told to only drink water the day of and that's exactly what she been doing. After her shower, Moisha began to put on a black romper with her red rainbows; she was beyond nervous. She knew the process was going to hurt; she just hoped it didn't hurt that bad. After she was ready, she finished the bottle of Aquafina water then disposed of it. She grabbed her purse and headed out the door. She headed out in the hallway and seen the man from Walmart.

"Afternoon, small world... or small Jackson," he said and Moisha laughed. Soon, he joined in.

"Dayquan, Quan, Day-day. Whatever you prefer," Dayquan said, introducing himself.

"I'm Moisha... can I say that your eyes are sooo beautiful," Moisha said, looking at him in his eyes, in particular. Moisha didn't know how good hazel eyes could look on a chocolate man.

"Thanks Moisha, you must have just moved here because I've never seen you around," he said and Moisha nodded.

"Yeah, I just moved like last week from Memphis," Moisha explained.

"Memphis Tennessee? Chocolate city?" he said with a laugh.

Moisha nodded. "Yup, yup." "But look, I'll catch you later. I have an appointment that I cannot be late for," Moisha told him and before he let her go, he gave her a flyer. As Moisha went to the parking deck, she looked at it. It was a flyer for Spoken Word at this coffee shop. Moisha was never really into Spoken Word but she figured it wouldn't kill her to go. It was tomorrow night and Moisha made it in her plans to go.

Once Moisha got into her car, she put the address for the clinic in her GPS then left in route. It took no longer than thirty minutes. Moisha swerved into the parking lot, soon parking in one of the many open spaces. For some odd reason, Moisha couldn't get out the driver's seat; it was as if something was holding her back. Moisha exhaled looking down at her flat tummy and as she did so, a tear escaped. She was about to kill her unborn child but it was better for the child because she didn't want it to be born in this mess she was in at all.

Moisha cut the car off then got up. After locking the doors, she began walking to the doors. The farther she walked, the distance to the door became longer. Moisha swallowed the lump in her throat as she went in. She went to sign her name on the sign in sheet and took a seat. Posted all over the place were facts about, abortions, safe sex, and diseases. Moisha didn't want to look at none of it so instead, she held her head down.

"Moisha Thomas?" someone said from a cracked door.

Moisha looked up to see a woman with a clipboard in her hand. She followed the lady to a vacant room. "Here for an abortion?" the lady asked and Moisha nodded, feeling as if this is what she had to do.

To be continued…

Made in the USA
Middletown, DE
13 July 2017